He stood in front of her.

"Always there, aren't you, Con?" he asked. "For a minute, I thought you were a shadow."

"I'm real, Duval," Connie said, holding out her arm. "Want to touch?"

One corner of his mouth turned up. "That could be dangerous."

"I don't think I have anything to worry about. You're not the type to take advantage of a woman."

"I'm not going to talk to you, you know. Following me isn't going to help. If anything, it's getting tiresome."

"Afraid I'll wear you down?" she asked, her low voice throbbing with challenge.

He shook his head. His eyes were filled with heat. "You don't scare me, Connie Kenyon. But I should scare you."

"Oh? Why is that, Duval? Are you dangerous?"

"With the right woman I can be," he murmured, his eyes caressing her face. "And you just might be the right woman."

Dear Reader,

Excitement is in the air at Harlequin! We're about to bring you some rousing new stories. Next month you'll not only notice a different look to your American Romance novels, you'll notice something new between the covers, too.

If you've ever dreamed of sailing the high seas with a swashbuckling modern-day pirate . . . riding off into the sunset with a dark and dangerous man on the back of a motorcycle . . . lassoing a cowboy Casanova and branding him your own . . . then the new American Romance is for you.

Fall in love with our bold American heroes, the sexiest men in the world. They'll take you on adventures that make their dreams—and yours—come true.

Your favorite American Romance authors will be on hand, as well as some fresh exciting voices.

So join us next month for the adventure of a lifetime!

Debra Matteucci
Senior Editor & Editorial Coordinator
Harlequin Books
300 E. 42nd St., 6th floor
New York, NY 10017

KATHERINE RANSOM

OUT OF HER LEAGUE

Harlequin Books

TORONTO • NEW YORK • LONDON
AMSTERDAM • PARIS • SYDNEY • HAMBURG
STOCKHOLM • ATHENS • TOKYO • MILAN
MADRID • WARSAW • BUDAPEST • AUCKLAND

Published August 1992

ISBN 0-373-16450-5

OUT OF HER LEAGUE

Chapter One

"Put some towels around you!" Charlie Huff shouted, as he escorted Connie Kenyon into the Boston Barons clubhouse. "There's a lady present."

The sports editor of the *Boston Courier*, Charlie Huff, was short and stout, with a beefy red face and a smelly cigar clamped between square white teeth. His announcement was greeted with whistles and cheers and banging on lockers by various members of the Boston Barons baseball team. A wet towel flew through the air and hit Charlie in the face.

"Hey, Huff!" someone called out. "You finally find a girlfriend?"

"She's no friend of mine," Charlie shouted back. "She's a reporter. Writes the society column. Listen up, guys. First thing you know, she'll want you to pose for afternoon tea at the Copley Plaza with watercress sandwiches and your pinkies in the air."

"Which pinky is that?" someone shouted.

This was met with guffaws and laughter, and Connie Kenyon found herself wishing Charlie hadn't bothered to "help" her. She looked around and wondered if it had been such a good idea to invade this utterly male territory. She'd never seen so many gorgeous male bodies in so few clothes in her life. She felt her face turn pink as someone let out a low, appreciative wolf whistle.

"My pinky's in the air!" someone shouted, and the locker room degenerated into catcalls and whistles and more pounding on the lockers.

She almost rolled her eyes. They weren't men; they were boys, loud and rude and obnoxious. She was reminded of junior high, when the boys used to stand outside the girls' gym and whistle and make faces when the girls walked by in their gym shorts. Not that she had to worry about these men making faces at her. With her platinum blond hair and deep blue eyes, Connie was used to men making passes at her. It came with the territory.

A white-haired assistant coach with a beer belly and tobacco-stained teeth stepped forward. "Name's McGillicuddy," he said politely, offering her a hand that looked like half a side of beef."But everyone calls me Millie. What can we do for you, ma'am?"

"I'd just like to look around and maybe talk to a few players," Connie said, shaking his hand.

"Anyone in particular?"

She hesitated only a moment. There was only one Barons player reporters wanted to talk to. She wouldn't be here if it weren't for his insistence on not talking to reporters.

"I'd like to speak to Jed Duval," she said, "but I hear he doesn't give interviews. Is that true?"

"'Fraid so, ma'am," Millie said, taking off his hat and scratching his head. "Jed's kinda publicity shy, I guess."

"Is there any special reason for that?"

Millie aimed a spurt of tobacco juice at an ashtray. It landed on the floor with a splat. "Not that I ever heard. 'Course, the way things are now, there's a million stories circulating about him. The tabloids make 'em up, but Jed just ignores 'em."

"Do you think these stories are why he refuses to speak with reporters?"

"Who knows? Could be. Jed's real quiet about his life. He'd give you the shirt off his back, but he don't volunteer much information about himself. At first it was kinda hard to understand, but now we accept it. That's just Jed. As long as he keeps pitching like he's been pitchin,' no one's gonna say anything."

"He seems to have been exactly what the team needed. Everyone said you would have won the World Series last year if he'd been able to pitch the last game."

"It sure seemed that way, anyway," the coach agreed. "If he hadn't had a sore arm, he would've pitched and we'd've probably won. But we couldn't take any chances. Not with *that* arm.''

''But no one can really say that with any certainty,'' Connie said. ''I mean, he could have pitched and lost.''

''Be the first time,'' the coach said, grinning. ''He's undefeated since he came up from the minors.''

''That must put a lot of pressure on him.''

''If it does, he sure don't show it. That man's the coolest I've ever seen in my forty years in baseball. Day of the game, he's like a machine—well oiled and ready to pitch. No emotions. He just rears back and throws heaters like it was the easiest thing in the world.''

''Yes, he does make it look that way, doesn't he?''

The coach shook his head admiringly. ''Wish we had a dozen more just like him—don't care if he talks to reporters or not.''

''Well, thanks so much. It's been helpful talking to you.''

''My pleasure,'' Millie said, touching his cap and ambling toward the office.

Connie turned to look for Jed Duval. She tried to ignore the ball players who called out to each other, threw towels and whistled appreciatively as she walked by. She felt nervous flutters in her midsection. Jed Duval had come up from the minor leagues at the beginning of last season and proceeded to win every game he'd pitched to a decision. With a record of 26 and 0, he'd turned baseball on its ear. Pitchers had to lose some of the games they pitched; the odds said so. But Jed Duval had defied the odds, making him the most talked-about athlete in the country. Now she was going to try her hand at getting an interview where every other reporter in the country had failed.

For as long as she could remember, Constance Kenyon had wanted to be a reporter. When she'd landed the job as the *Boston Courier*'s society reporter, she thought she'd at last fulfilled her dream. Now she knew better. In three short years she'd become the society editor, but on the *Courier* that cut about as much mustard as a dull knife. She was little more than an object of derision in the newsroom.

But things were about to change. For over a year now, she'd listened to Charlie Huff and the other sports reporters gripe about Duval—about how he didn't give interviews, wouldn't talk, wouldn't even share a beer with them after a game. Quietly, she'd gone about digging into Duval's past. She'd come up with nothing. The blank pages had intrigued her. He hadn't just sprung from a rock; he had to have come from somewhere. She was determined to find out. She was nervous, but knew it was time to make her move. Thankfully, her editor had agreed with her that a woman might be able to get the story that a bunch of men couldn't.

She found Duval in the farthest corner of the locker room. He stood in front of his locker, his chest bare, a pair of faded jeans riding low on his lean hips. She couldn't help it; her eyes traveled admiringly down his body and up again. In a room full of nearly naked men, Jed Duval stood out. His swarthy skin was so dark it looked like he had some sort of foreign blood running in his veins—Mexican, she guessed, or perhaps Italian. His upper body rippled with finely developed muscles. His shoulders were big and broad, the kind of shoulders that looked like they could hold up a brick building. His upper arms were sculpted with sinews and muscles. His muscular chest was sprinkled with curly black hair that tapered into a vee and disappeared into the waistband of his jeans.

But it wasn't just his physical appearance that caught her eye. The other players cavorted around the room, playing practical jokes on each other, shouting, swearing, laughing and pushing each other good-naturedly. In contrast, Duval was self-contained, almost aloof. He was as quiet and watchful as a wild animal sensing danger. An aura of power surrounded him. He wasn't a man who would be frightened easily. And though he wouldn't back down from a fight, he wouldn't start one either.

Connie stood watching him, wondering what had happened in his life to give him this magnetic quality. Any of the other men might be interesting; Jed Duval was riveting. There was something almost frightening about him, a combination, she supposed, of his size, his dark skin and the aura of power that surrounded him.

He turned, then, and saw her. She shook off the apprehension that shot through her and whispered a prayer of thanks to the gods that she wasn't shaking. "Mr. Duval," she said, "could I talk to you a moment?"

He dipped his head in an old-fashioned, courteous mannerism she found charming. "Yes, ma'am," he said politely, "what can I do for you?"

His voice was low, and when she drew closer she saw that his eyes were a startling gray, filled with warmth. She felt a strange shock, as if she'd touched a live wire with damp hands. She found herself unable to speak. She stood and looked into his eyes, momentarily mesmerized by the fact that he wasn't aloof and cold at all, nor even frightening. Instead, he seemed gentle. His eyes were as warm as the sun; they seemed to burn into hers.

A small smile played at his lips. "You said you wanted to speak with me," he reminded her gently.

"Yes." She mentally girded herself for his reaction when he found out who she was. "Mr. Duval, is it true that you refuse to speak to reporters?"

He studied her with speculative eyes. "Yes, ma'am, that's correct."

"Why is that?" she asked.

He cocked his head. "Why? Are you a reporter?"

"Yes, Mr. Duval," she said, reluctantly handing him her card. "I am. Connie Kenyon from the *Boston Courier*."

He studied the card, then looked up at her. She almost stepped back she was so startled at the change in his face. Where his eyes had been warm just seconds ago, they were now cold, as forbidding as the Boston sky in a winter storm.

She had the oddest feeling he was about to bolt. She wanted to ask her questions before he got away. "I heard you donated a hundred thousand dollars to the Catholic archdiocese for the orphanage they run," she said hurriedly.

He didn't say a word, just pulled on a chambray shirt and began buttoning it.

"Mr. Duval," she said softly, "I'd just like to talk to you. I promise I'd give you complete approval rights to any story I wrote. Nothing would hit the papers that you hadn't first seen and approved of. I'd stand right next to you while you read it. Surely that's fair."

"I'm sorry, Ms. Kenyon, but I don't speak with reporters." With that, he slammed his locker door and strode away, leaving Connie staring after him, shocked and miffed at the sudden change in him.

From behind her, Charlie Huff said in a singsong voice: "I told you so."

"What's with this guy?" she asked.

"Beats me."

"There has to be a reason he won't talk to the press."

Charlie smiled smugly. "Make a good story, wouldn't it?"

"A darned good one," she said, staring after Duval.

"Now you see why it bugs me and every other sportswriter in the country. I want that story so bad I wake up at night, unable to sleep. Jed Duval haunts me. Sometimes I think I'd kill for that story."

She glanced at Charlie, wondering just how far he'd go to get the story. At least now she understood him better. Having experienced Jed Duval's reaction when he'd found out what she was, she understood the itch of curiosity, could imagine what it must be like to feel that itch day after day, month after month. It would begin to eat at a person, the way it was eating at Charlie Huff.

"Do you know anything about him?"

Charlie shrugged. "Not much. He's an enigma. I can't even find out where he went to high school. He seems to have come out of nowhere. Showed up at a summer camp one day with a smoking fastball and was signed the same day. He played Class A ball for a few years, then the Barons got him in a trade. Worked in Double A ball for a couple years, then went on to Triple A. The Barons finally brought him up a year ago and you know what happened then. He was like a light being turned on—he's been shining ever since."

"But surely the Barons know something about him," Connie said.

"Yeah, but facts are sparse as hens' teeth. His bio says he was born in Waco, Texas. Period. When I asked the general manager if Jed played high school or college ball, he just said not to his knowledge." Charlie met Connie's eyes. "You know the chances of a guy getting to the big leagues who didn't at least pitch high-school ball?"

Connie shook her head.

"Almost nil," Charlie answered. "It just doesn't happen. A kid learns to play ball in Little League, and if he's a natural he just gets better. By the time he's in high school, most scouts already know about him." Charlie shook his head. "But this guy is baffling. Makes you wonder what kind of skeletons he's hiding in his closet."

"Who says there have to be skeletons?" Connie said. "Maybe he just dislikes publicity."

"Uh-uh," Charlie said, shaking his head. "I'd bet my life on this one, Con. The guy's hiding something. I feel it in my bones, and my bones are never wrong."

"There's always a first time, Charlie."

"Not this time," Charlie countered. "But you go ahead and poke around. See if you come up with something. I guarantee you, something's fishy with the guy. I dunno, maybe he was in prison or something. In trouble with the law, that kind of thing."

"But if that were true, someone would remember him and come forward. You know how people are about celebrities, Charlie. If they've known someone who gets famous, they want to capitalize on it."

"True," Charlie said, then sighed. "It doesn't make sense. Something just doesn't smell right to me."

"You've been standing around locker rooms too long," Connie said, grinning. "Maybe you just need a little fresh air."

SHE CAUGHT UP WITH Duval in the parking lot behind Barons Field where players and Barons office personnel parked their cars. She smiled to herself as she noted what he drove—a four-wheel-drive vehicle, either a Bronco or Blazer, she couldn't tell which from this distance. So. What did that make him? A typical yuppie trying to make his life look like a Ralph Lauren ad, or a rifle-toting, hard-drinking good ole boy with a couple bird dogs waiting at home and a six-pack stashed under the dash?

"Mr. Duval," she called, regretting that she was wearing three-inch heels as she tried to catch up with him. "Please, I just want to talk with you."

To her surprise, he turned and waited for her. He leaned back against the Blazer—she made a mental note to jot down what it was—and waited as she approached him. His eyes were filled with something that looked an awful lot like admiration as she walked up to him.

"Thanks for waiting," she said when she reached him. She smiled at him. "I thought you didn't talk to reporters."

"Most reporters don't look like you," he said, his eyes filled with quiet amusement.

"Then I guess I have an advantage."

He smiled crookedly, one corner of his sculpted mouth lifting humorously. "As a woman you do. I wouldn't put odds on your chances as a reporter."

"Charlie Huff thinks you're hiding something," she said without preamble, her eyes trained directly on him to study his reaction. "Are you?"

He sighed and pushed away from the truck. "Look, I just don't want any stories written about me, okay? I'm a quiet man who likes his privacy. End of explanation." He turned to open the door of the Blazer.

Without even thinking, Connie reached out and put a hand on his arm. "Don't go," she said urgently. "Please."

He stopped as if he'd been hit, becoming as still as a rattlesnake about to strike. He lifted his gray eyes and met her gaze and she felt herself grow almost faint. The wind kicked up and blew her blond hair across her eyes and carefully, as if in slow motion, he reached out and brushed it back from her face.

She looked up at him, her lips parted, her eyes drowning in his. She felt some sort of elemental surge of attraction lift inside her, felt herself floating in his eyes, swimming in them, groundless, pliant, taken away by a current over which she had no control. Time stopped and the breeze died away and nothing existed for a second but Jed Duval and his incredible eyes.

It happened as quickly as that—contact. Swift, inevitable, undeniable, like an electric charge sending sparks between the two of them. Then he stepped back and the contact was broken. She looked away, feeling a rush of pink color flood her cheeks. She couldn't speak, wouldn't have known what to say even if she could.

"Sorry, Miss Kenyon," he said in a low voice. "I just don't talk to reporters."

That galvanized her. She felt determination shoot through her, hot and salty, like the taste of blood on her lips. "I'm not going to give up, Duval," she said. "I'm going to be on you like butter on toast."

He looked back, that corner of his mouth lifting in amusement. "Nice image. It's almost too tempting to resist."

"Then why try?" she asked, her eyes riveted on his, daring him.

He let out a sigh and shook his head. "Some other time, maybe. When you don't have a reporter's notebook strapped to your thigh."

"You make me sound like a gunslinger."

"Mmm, hmm," he said, his eye filled with something like contempt, "loaded for bear and out for blood."

"That's not what I want," she said. "I'm not out to do a hatchet job on you. I just want to write about you."

"Why? What's so important about writing about me?" He tilted his head consideringly, his eyes boring into hers. There was no mistaking it now—it was contempt she saw in those gray eyes, hard and condemning, and he didn't even know her. "You out to make a name for yourself, Connie Kenyon? You want to be the one who gets the story no other reporter could get?"

She was taken aback at his insight. "What's wrong with that, Duval? You must understand ambition. You've worked hard to get where you are."

"That's why I won't talk with you. People like you are dangerous, Miss Kenyon. You forget what's really important in your quest for fame."

"And you never have?" she taunted softly.

A muscle worked in his cheek. His eyes were filled with something cold, ugly almost. "That's right," he said, turning. "I never have."

He was gone before she could stop him, cranking up the engine and backing out of his parking place like a man chased by the devil. The gravel in the parking lot kicked up under his wheels and he roared off in an explosion of ignition and exhaust fumes.

She stood and stared after him, determined. Nothing was going to stop her from getting this story. This was a grudge thing now.

Chapter Two

Over the next two weeks, Connie was relentless. She was at Barons Field every day, seated in the bleachers or behind the catcher's box, her binoculars trained on Duval as he warmed up in the bull pen or took batting practice. She attended every home game, got a temporary press pass and invaded the clubhouse after every game. Eventually, she began to feel at ease in this utterly male territory.

She ate and slept Duval, filling up on the stories about him in *Sports Illustrated* and *Time,* in the *Sporting News,* and the *Courier*'s crosstown rivals, the *Globe* and the *Herald.* Duval was disgustingly normal in his life-style. If Connie hadn't met him, she'd have said he was boring. He lived in a small town house in a suburb of Boston. He had a housekeeper who bought his groceries at the local supermarket and who refused to talk to Connie. He jogged and worked out on weight equipment in the Barons' weight room.

He occasionally drank a couple of beers after a game with some of the other players in a local bar, but always made it home in time for curfew. Connie had even lowered herself to going through his garbage. It was matter-of-fact and unrevealing—a wrapper off a roll of paper towels, an empty box of Cheerios, a few pieces of junk mail, unopened, and not much else.

She hounded the other players on the Barons, peering intently at them as they stood in the locker room with towels draped around their taut middles, her notebook in hand as she jotted down notes.

"Duval just doesn't like reporters," Larry Connors, the Barons' first string catcher said. "Give the guy a break. Now me, you can follow me around and write anything about me you want."

"Jed's a nice guy," Rinaldo Pinoza said. "So what if he don't want to talk to the papers? He pitches like the wind. I never seen anyone work harder than Jed. Never. And I been in the majors thirteen years."

"The guy's charmed," Danny Campbell said. Danny was a pitcher with the Barons. "You know how utterly impossible it is to win every game you pitch in a single year? Then to come back the next year and start doing it all over again?" He shook his head. "Impossible. It can't be done. But he's done it. He's doing it." He shook his head again. "The guy's charmed, I tell you. He's simply incredible."

Everything she heard made her want the story even more. Tension gripped her. She began to have trouble sleeping. She found herself waking up in the early morning hours with his face imprinted on her consciousness. She began to dream about him. One morning she woke up from a particularly disturbing dream—Duval had taken her by the hand and led her to the pitcher's mound, where he began to make love to her in front of a packed stadium at Baron's Field. What was really disturbing was that she'd been enjoying it....

SHE WENT ACROSS TOWN to Fenway Park and interviewed Buzz Drummond, a former National League player who'd just been traded to the American League Red Sox. In her research, she'd found that Buzz Drummond had played in the minor leagues with Jed. He was lounging near the batting cage at Fenway Park when Connie found him, chewing a wad of bubble gum and razzing the hitter taking batting practice.

Buzz Drummond did a double take when he saw Connie. "Well, hello," he said, taking off his cap and breaking into an appreciative grin. "You drop out of heaven, or did Boston just get lucky?"

Connie smiled. Ball players, she was fast finding out, were a colorful lot, and they made no bones about how much they liked an attractive woman. Buzz Drummond had bright red hair and a face full of freckles. His green eyes leaped with mischief.

She handed him her card. "I wonder if I could talk to you a minute?"

He looked up from her card, his grin huge. "Sure thing. I got the next twenty-thirty years free."

"Mr. Drummond—"

"Aw, heck, call me Buzz. Everyone does but my mom, and she refuses to call me anything but Elmer."

"All right, Buzz," Connie said. "I was wondering if I could talk to you about Jed Duval?"

"You and every other reporter in the country. Sorry, ma'am, but I don't know much about him, 'cept he's the best damn pitcher in the game right now."

"But you played with him in the minors."

"Played with him the first year out, back in Class A ball. I got traded then and ended up hitting against him. Scared the devil out of me, first time I was up against him. He used to rear back and throw that ball so it looked like a locomotive coming right at you. Sounded like a tornado swooping down on Kansas. He threw like the devil himself, but couldn't pitch worth beans."

"What's the big difference between throwing and pitching?" she asked.

"Pitchers got moves. They know how to hold the ball, aim it, they control it, make it do what they want. Throwers like Jed was when he first came up, they just rear back and throw heat. They don't know how to control the ball, make it break when they want, slow it down, that kind of thing."

"But Jed Duval has learned that."

"You bet he has," Buzz said, grinning widely. "I hear up in Triple A ball, he painted a bull's-eye on an old barn and he'd be out there first thing every morning, throwing against the barn. Heard first time out he broke the first board he hit. Had to reinforce it all in the back. They say that old bull's-eye's still there, and the board behind the exact center is dented from all the times he hit it with the force of his throw."

Connie was thankful she knew shorthand. She had the quote down exactly, but wondered if she'd ever get a story she could use it in. "Where exactly is that old barn?" she asked.

"Beats me," Buzz said, blowing a huge bubble. "Somebody told me it don't even exist, it's just a story." He scratched his head. "But I dunno, it kinda sounds like Jed to me. He's driven, got a fire in his belly. Nice and gentle off the field, but on that mound, he's a tiger. Looks down off the mound and those eyes of his make you shake in your cleats."

"Is that part of what makes him unbeatable? The fear he inspires?"

"Yeah, that's part of it, sure. Any pitcher with a decent fastball can throw so fast you feel like you never see the ball, but a good pitcher with real control can brush the batter back, make him afraid to lean over and get a piece of the plate. Duval used to depend on throwing hard and fast. Now he's got control, too, so he's got everything covered.

"You're standing up there and you sometimes can't even see the damn ball—looks like a pea flying by you—but then you hear it hit the catcher's mitt and you shiver a little. Whup! Like a comet hitting earth at a million miles an hour. I heard old Larry actually grunt last year when I was up at bat. He told me later his hands hurt for two days after catching for Jed."

"Larry?"

"Larry Connors, the Barons' catcher." Buzz Drummond grinned. "You don't follow baseball much, do you?"

"I'm a fan," Connie said, smiling, "but I don't usually write about sports. You'll have to bear with me."

"Any time, Miss Kenyon. Any time, any place, anywhere."

She smiled wryly. "I sure wish Jed Duval had your attitude."

Buzz shook his head. "Doubt that'll happen any time soon. He used to stay away from reporters even in the minors. Never seemed to have time for 'em. Just baseball. He lived it and ate it, and I imagine he slept it." Buzz grinned and fell into step beside Connie as she made her way toward the gate. "Hell, I remember how I used to cut out every news story that had my name in it, collect them all in a big scrapbook I sent home to my mom. Not Jed. Just smiled and went about his business, and Jed Duval's business is baseball."

"What about women?" Connie asked. Duval has the look of a man who drew women like a magnet. That deadly aura of power and danger was a potent aphrodisiac. For some reason, she didn't especially want to find out about this aspect of Jed's life, but she was a reporter first, a woman second.

"Women?" Buzz Drummond smiled lazily. "Jed likes 'em well enough. Hell, they fell all over him every town he was in, but he never spent a lot of time chasing after them. He had a girlfriend for a while, but she got tired of him being gone all the time and up and married her high-school sweetheart. Actually, Jed's kinda shy around women. Courteous. Old-fashioned, almost."

"Where was this?" Connie asked.

"That'd be down in Texas. Jed was playing on a Double A team then."

"Do you remember her name, by any chance?"

Buzz screwed up his face and thought about it. "Laurie? Laura?" He shook his head. "Pretty girl. Blond hair, blue eyes. Just an all-American girl with freckles on her nose. Sweet, too." He screwed up his face, as if he were searching his memory, and suddenly brightened. "Laureen Denver! Yessir. Laureen. Married a guy named John Bob Jenkins. I 'member his name cuz it sounded like a typical good ole boy from Texas, and that's what John Bob was. How Laureen could have settled for him after she'd been with Jed is beyond me." He scratched his head as if puzzled. "Oh, well, never have understood women."

Connie ignored the comment. "Do you know where she was from?"

"Let's see, as I remember, Laureen was from a little town called Bumpus, near Sweetwater. She's livin' there still, I'd bet, married to John Bob Jenkins with a passel of kids."

"OH, SURE, I REMEMBER Jed," Laureen Jenkins said on the phone the next day. "He was a real sweet guy. I always knew he'd make something of himself. Just crazy about pitching."

Laureen sighed. "Jed was my first love," she said softly, "and you know how that is—heart palpitations and wet palms—but I knew he wasn't a marrying man. He wasn't ever going to settle down till he got the fire out in his gut—"

"The fire in his gut?"

"His desire to play in the big leagues. It consumed him, just ate at him. He was a driven man, Miss Kenyon, and a woman like me needs a man she can count on." She smiled. "Like my husband. He's given me three wonderful kids. I wouldn't give them up for all the fame in the world. Anyway..." She paused, and Con got the feeling she was struggling with something, as if maybe she didn't know whether she should say something.

"Yes, Mrs. Jenkins?" Con prompted gently.

Laureen hesitated. "Jed's a good man. Decent. I wish him the best."

Con knew she'd lost her. She tried again, anyway. "Could you tell me anything about him, Mrs. Jenkins? Where he grew up? Did he have family? Friends?"

"Jed never talked about any family. He told me he'd moved from town to town when he was young, just he and his dad. I think it was his dad taught him how to play baseball. His mother died when he was born. She was Mexican. He never spoke about her, except just that one time when I asked him."

Mexican. So she'd been right about part of his heritage.

"How do you feel, now that Jed's famous? Do you ever think of the times when you were dating him?"

Laureen smiled, and Connie could feel that smile across a thousand miles of telephone wires. "Oh, yeah, sometimes I remember what it was like bein' with him. Lord, he was a man! In those days, I cared about a man bein' in shape, and Jed Duval was *in shape*, let me tell you! And kiss! Lord, I liked to died when he took me in his arms that first time and kissed me. Nearly fainted, it was so wonderful!" Laureen giggled softly. "But that's my little secret, Miss Kenyon, it's what I take out when I'm awake late at night and can't sleep, like takin' a locket out of an old jewel case. I remember fallin' in love with Jed Duval, and being held by him. But I was a young girl, then, Miss

Kenyon, and Jed was a boy. We weren't meant for each other. It took John Bob Jenkins to show me that.''

"So you have no regrets?" Connie asked softly.

"Not even a one," Laureen Jenkins said. "I got the best of both worlds—my memories of Jed and a life with John Bob and my girls.''

CONNIE DROVE ACROSS TOWN to Barons Field and took a seat in the stands. Sometimes it helped just to sit and soak up the atmosphere of a place. She often felt as if she had antennae which were always turning here and there, focusing on a person or group, tuning in to them and what they were saying, noting it all in some subliminal spot in her unconscious, and then moving on, always noticing details, observing rites and social niceties, like a visitor from another planet.

She smiled grimly to herself. In a way, that's exactly what she was. She didn't like to think about the place she'd come from, but it was a long way from Boston's Beacon Hill.

"What's up, Constance Kenyon?" a voice asked from nearby. "Wishing you were back on your society beat, munching cookies at the Copley Plaza?''

She looked up to find Charlie Huff standing over her, his eyes filled with cynical amusement. She smiled to herself. The joke was on Charlie, though he'd never know it.

"Actually, Charlie, I was enjoying the smell of the ballpark."

"Slumming," he said, sitting down next to her. He sighed and stretched his legs out. "A woman can never understand baseball the way a man can."

It was her turn to smile cynically. "No?"

He shook his head. "Baseball's a man's game. It's in our blood. Sometimes I sit here in the stands, watching the players take BP, and I get this holy feeling, better than when I'm in church." He shook his head again. "No, there's no place like a ballpark. Heroes play this game, and little boys come and watch them, their eyes wide and hearts filled with dreams." He sighed and put his head back to catch the sun. "You'd never be able to understand that."

But she did. She remembered her father watching the Sox, remembered the excitement in his voice when Carl Yazstremski hit a home run or Rico Petrocelli made a sliding catch at third, remembered the tears that welled up in his sentimental Irish eyes when the national anthem was played, the way he talked about Ted Williams and Dom DeMaggio and Jimmy Piersall, as if they were indeed gods walking on the earth, men larger than life who somehow made his own joyless life slightly more bearable.

There was something about baseball that lifted you above the normal earthly cares. She always felt it when she sat in a ballpark, felt the presence of something almost ineffable, as if the very air were laden with sad men's dreams, with the remembrance of youth and the knowledge of death. You sat in the stands and for a few hours lived in a golden world where one man could change the destiny of an entire team, where any man could matter for a day.

She felt her throat close up, but she knew she could never tell Charlie Huff what she felt, could never convince him that a woman could feel these feelings too, could know the joy that such a supposedly simple game as baseball could bring to a defeated life. She knew baseball wasn't just a game, it was bigger than that. It was about dreams and despair, winning and losing, heroes and charlatans.

She felt tears spring into her eyes and she was glad she was wearing sunglasses, because she could never in a million years convince a man like Charlie Huff that she understood. He thought only a man knew these feelings. She knew women could feel them too. They just didn't talk about them all that much, worn down as most women were by children and housework and making a living and tending to the needs of others.

"Jed's out in the bull pen today," Charlie Huff said. "Resting his arm. You won't get near him now, you know. He knows who you are. It was stupid to tell him, Con. You coulda capitalized on being a woman."

"So what do you think I should have done, Charlie? Sleep with him to get my story?"

Charlie shrugged. "Why not? You'll do that eventually, anyway."

She stared at him, remembering suddenly the dream she'd had about Jed Duval. "Good grief, Charlie, I will not!"

"Oh, come on, Con, I've seen you lookin' at him. You think no one's watching, your eyes devour him."

She felt a surge of color fill her face. "That's ridiculous!"

He sat back, stretching out his short, stubby legs and lifting his face again to the sun. "Sex, Con, I can smell it a mile away. You two get alone for even a minute, he'll be tearing your clothes off your back."

The color drained out of her face, leaving her shaking. "That's...absurd..."

Charlie chuckled. "Hey, it had to happen sometime. Duval's been in Boston a year now and he hasn't had a girlfriend that I've been able to find. I see him lookin' at you, Con—his eyes smolder. Looks like a fire's burning in 'em way in the back. Makes me think of that movie—what was it? *Fatal Attraction?*" He grinned at the sick look on her face. "Hey, you two come together, it'd be like water hitting a hot griddle."

"Charlie, I'm a reporter!"

"So? You think I wouldn't do anything to get a story on Duval? Why shouldn't you? You're hungry, Con. I can tell. You've got the look. You want that story so bad you can taste it. You'd sell your soul for this story.'' He grinned wolfishly. "So do what you gotta do, kid. You convinced Vinnie a woman might be able to get the story I couldn't. Go for it."

She shook her head. "Not that way, Charlie. Never that way."

Charlie smiled, his eyes closed, his face still turned to the sun. "Why not? It's perfectly respectable. Other women reporters do it. Hell, I've even known a few men to do it, if it meant a good story."

"You're sick, Charlie," she said, standing up. "Let me by."

He opened his eyes and peered up at her, his eyes filled with cynical laughter. "Honey, you don't know what you'll do to get a story till it's crunch time. You wait. It'll begin to eat at you, a little at a time, until you won't know which you want most—Duval or the story. That's when you sleep with him. Just make sure you have a tape recorder, Con—it's the pillow talk that undoes 'em all the time."

She didn't bother to reply. She stepped over him and headed for the exit, her chin high. Damn Charlie Huff and his dirty little insinuations.

It was only when she was halfway to her car that she realized she was shaking, dazed by Charlie's revelations, as if he'd slapped her across the face to wake her up.

Chapter Three

Connie flung down her pen and rubbed her eyes. She flexed her shoulders, trying to get the kinks out of them. She'd been rewriting press releases for hours and it was now past six o'clock. Somewhere in the bowels of the building, the *Boston Courier* was churning off the presses, page after page of newsprint filled with millions of words, stories about the economy and foreign affairs, local politics and police-blotter news, cartoons and editorials, advertisements and want ads.

About the only thing that wouldn't be in the next day's edition was a story about Jed Duval. Connie slid lower in her chair and stared moodily out the window into a brick-lined air shaft in mid-Boston. After three weeks, she still had nothing on Duval.

She turned back to the pile of papers on her desk that remained to be read. Lots of press releases, some invitations to dinners, meetings, society openings. A letter from the board of education in Waco, Texas: "I regret that we are unable to find any record of a Jed Duval having attended any school in Waco.''

She scanned the rest of the mail, then noticed a press release at the bottom of the pile. It was an announcement by the Orphan Society that they were holding a Charity Bachelor Auction next week. It had been sitting unnoticed in her ''in'' basket under the incoming mail for three weeks. She was ready to rewrite it for Friday's paper when a sentence jumped off the page at her: *"Among the bachelors participating in the Charity Bachelor Auction are Boston Barons pitcher Jed Duval..."*

She devoured the rest of the press release: ''Duval will accompany the winning bidder to a remote island off the coast of Maine for a relaxing weekend that starts with a leisurely drive to Maine on Friday afternoon, crossing on a ferry to Mr. Duval's private island, where he will personally prepare a fabulous fresh fish dinner that evening. He promises fresh air, sunshine, the opportunity to unwind and relax in peace and privacy. As with all our bachelor offerings, Mr. Duval's package provides for separate rooms.''

Connie lifted her head, excitement racing through her like greyhounds after prey. This was it—the break she'd been waiting for. All she had to do was attend the bachelor auction, outbid everyone else, and Jed Duval would be hers for an entire weekend. He'd have to talk to her then.

"I'VE GOT HIM NOW!" Connie said when she burst into Vinnie Carbone's office waving the press release.

"Got who?" Vinnie said, sitting back. He was a morose-faced man with a receding hairline and deep worry lines permanently etched into his forehead. He drank Mylanta by the bottle but insisted on eating spicy food. The remains of a Chinese meal sat in little white paper cartons on his desk, making the place smell more like Hong Kong than the office of the editor-in-chief of the *Boston Courier*.

"Jed Duval." She thrust the press release under Vinnie's nose. "Here. Read it yourself."

He took the paper and scanned it. "Bidding is encouraged to start in the five-hundred-dollar range," he read out aloud, then raised sad eyes to hers. "I suppose you're going to want the money to bid for Duval?"

"I'll have him alone for an entire weekend that way, Vinnie. A thousand dollars should do it," she answered.

"A thousand bucks!" Vinnie stared at her like she needed professional help. "Jeez, Con, money doesn't grow on trees around here, you know."

"Come on, Vinnie," she said, "you've got the money. All I have to do is outbid the competition. We'll spend the entire weekend together on an island off Maine. Even Jed Duval won't be able to be quiet for two whole days."

Vinnie sat with his chin in his hand, staring at the floor, then he shrugged. "What the hell? Go for it. Even if you don't come up with any information, you can still do a story about buying a weekend with the famous Jed Duval at the Charity Bachelor Auction."

"Vinnie, please," she said, rolling her eyes. "That's not the kind of story I want to write."

"Well that may be all you'll get to write, honey. You've been on this three weeks and you've got nothing to show for it. You want to break out of the society pages, you're gonna have to do better than this."

"All I have to do is spend some time alone with him and get him to open up."

"Sure, Con," Vinnie said sarcastically. "Like you're going to be the one who changes his mind about reporters."

She stared at him, realizing he had real doubts about her. "I'll get the story, Vinnie," she said quietly. "I promise you."

"Fine. See that you do. Otherwise you'll be back on society writing about volunteer organizations for the rest of your life."

"I promised Duval I wouldn't write anything without his approval," she said.

"Oh, jeez, Con," Vinnie said, throwing down the press release. "What are you telling me?"

"That I need to gain his trust, Vinnie. Jed Duval has to have a reason why he won't talk to reporters. Maybe he got burned sometime in the past. I'm not going to shaft him, Vinnie, or he'll never open up to anyone again."

"So what are you, Con, a social worker or a reporter? It's not your job to reassure the guy. Just bring in a story, or you'll be in Society till your retirement. And, Con—" Vinnie leaned over his desk toward her "—this is your shot. If you blow it, that's it for you."

HIS HERO WAS TED WILLIAMS. His favorite singers were Tina Turner and Steve Winwood. His favorite meal was fried clams. And according to the Barons' official yearbook, which she sat in the stadium reading, he didn't have a favorite book.

She threw the yearbook down onto the seat next to her and scanned the field as the players warmed up for tonight's game. This wasn't what she wanted to know about Jed Duval. She wanted to know him inside and out, good and bad, wretched and glorious. Because only then would she be able to write a story about him, something worth chopping down trees to make paper for. She wanted to get under his skin and into his blood, to see the world as he saw it. So that when she wrote that story everyone who read it would know Jed Duval, too, live in his shoes, understand him as they'd never understood anyone before.

She sighed and rubbed her eyes. Sometimes she grew tired of her desires; they exhausted her. Why did she have to have outsized ambitions, disorderly dreams? She wished she could be content with finding a man, having a child, making a home for her family. But she couldn't. Ambition stirred inside her like a beast in a deep, dark cave. It made her what she was.

Charlie Huff had told her a couple weeks back that she'd sell her soul to get this story she wanted so much. She wondered if Charlie was right.

Feeling restless, she went down to the clubhouse. She leaned against the wall near Duval's locker and watched him. She made no move to approach him, just stood perfectly still, so quiet he didn't even know she was there, her eyes fastened on him as if he were the answer to every question, the reason why she breathed.

His shirt was off, giving her an unencumbered view of his muscular back and arms. She felt herself responding to him despite her reminder that this was a job and Duval was just the subject of a story. In the past few weeks, she'd grown used to unclothed players in the clubhouse, but it was obvious that she hadn't grown accustomed to Jed Duval. A small but very pleasurable response to him churned in her midsection, making it increasingly difficult to keep her mind on business.

He was only a man, she told herself, just like all the others. Half the men on the Barons' roster had already jokingly propositioned her. If she'd wanted a date or a quick tumble in bed, she could have had her choice. But not one of the others affected her the way Jed Duval did.

Watching him, she found herself wondering about the seemingly lonely life he led. He didn't have a steady girlfriend—didn't even date casually, as far as she could tell. She'd actually followed him home a couple of times, had parked outside his condominium and waited for a woman to try to sneak out in the hours just before dawn. None had.

For a moment, she closed her eyes and let herself imagine what it would be like to be his girlfriend. She saw his smoldering gray eyes, saw his lips descending toward hers, imagined the feel of his lips on hers, felt their warmth, the way he moved his mouth over hers commandingly. The fantasy was so vivid, she began to tremble. A dull ache filled her, and a strange sense of loss and desolation swept over her. For some unfathomable reason, she envisioned a whistling wind whipping across a desolate prairie, and she knew that was what her life was like—empty, unpeopled, as barren as a desert.

She usually swept these kinds of thoughts away, but today, standing in the shadows of the Boston Barons' clubhouse, she couldn't get them out of her mind. Perhaps that was why Jed Duval fascinated her so much—she sensed that he was as lost and lonely as she was.

Opening her eyes, she found herself face-to-face with Duval. He stood in front of her, his gray eyes taking everything in. She felt immediately exposed, violated almost, as if she'd found him watching her undress.

"Always there, aren't you, Con?" he asked bitterly. "For a minute, I thought you were a shadow."

She straightened from the wall, sweeping all her private fears aside, taking refuge behind her professional facade. "I'm real, Duval," she said, holding out her arm. "Want to touch?"

One corner of his mouth turned up. "That could be dangerous."

"I don't think I have anything to worry about. I've been watching you long enough to know you're not the type to take advantage of a woman."

"I'm not going to talk to you, you know. I don't talk to reporters. Following me isn't going to help. If anything, it's getting tiresome."

"Afraid I'll wear you down?" she asked, her low voice throbbing with challenge.

He shook his head. His eyes were filled with heat. "You don't scare me, Connie Kenyon. But I should scare you."

"Oh? Why is that, Duval? Are you dangerous?"

"With the right woman, I can be," he murmured, his eyes caressing her face. "And you just might be the right woman."

She smiled knowingly. "I'm a reporter, Duval, your dreaded enemy. Aren't you afraid I'd use anything against you if you ever trusted me?"

"That's what Charlie Huff says," he said.

She felt as if her head had snapped back on her neck. Hot color flooded her face. "Charlie Huff thinks every woman reporter sleeps with men to get a story. Don't believe it, Duval. I don't have to use my body to do my job."

"That's disappointing," he murmured, his eyes filled with amusement. "I might have given you an interview just to sleep with you."

"You only wish," she said, pushing away from the wall. "Good luck out there tonight, Duval." She turned to go, then hesitated. "What's it like to feel everyone's eyes on you, game after game? Do you ever want to lose a game just to get them off your back?"

"'Them'?" He cocked his head. "Aren't you one of them? You reporters hover around, waiting for one misstep, then you'd be on me like flies on carrion."

She searched his eyes, dismayed to realize he thought of her in such an unflattering way. "I wouldn't betray you," she said, meeting his direct gaze. She felt a sense of urgency, as if convincing him of her trustworthiness was the most important thing she could ever do. "I don't want to hurt you, Duval, but you're a great story. People want to know about you. Someone else might make a hash of things, but I wouldn't."

He turned his head, as if he couldn't stand to look at her a moment longer. "I'm sorry, Con, but I won't change my mind."

"You'd like me to believe that," she said softly. "But look at you. You're talking to me now."

"Because I can't resist you," he murmured. "If you were anything in the world but a reporter, I'd ask you out in a minute."

Flushing, she looked down, suddenly needing an excuse to look busy. She fussed with her notebook, adjusted the strap on her bag. "I guess the fates are against us," she said, finally managing to meet his eyes again.

"Drop the assignment."

She looked into his eyes, seeing the desire in them, and for a minute she wished she could, but then her reporter's instinct kicked in and she found herself wondering if this was just his way of taking her off the scent. "I'm sorry," she said, backing away, "but I can't do that."

"Can't? Or won't."

She shrugged. "Does it matter?"

"I suppose not." Turning, he went back to his locker and began suiting up.

She felt a sudden urge to tell him she'd forget everything, that the story didn't matter, but deep inside she knew she'd be lying. Something drove her on, some strange desire she didn't even understand. Turning, she left the locker room.

What was happening to her? Why was Jed Duval so important? Maybe she should just turn her back on him and walk away. Maybe she had taken on more than she could handle.

Stubbornly, she pushed her doubts out of her mind. She bought a ticket for the game and found her seat in the stands near third base. It was early yet, the sun was still high enough in the sky to light the outfield.

Then Jed Duval took the field. He was a commanding presence on the mound, his hat pulled low over his eyes, black paint daubed like war paint under each eye, his jaw set, his eyes flinty. She reached for her binoculars and adjusted them, studying his face. She felt her heartbeat accelerate, felt goose bumps on her arms as he went into his stretch, his eyes steely as he looked down at the catcher sixty feet away.

He didn't know it yet, but she had him in her sights. Jed Duval might want to escape the eyes of the press, but he wasn't going to escape hers.

Chapter Four

Connie stepped off the elevator on the penthouse level of the spacious Hotel Commodore. She was greeted by the brain-rattling music of a rock-and-roll band and the sound of over five hundred laughing, chattering women. The Orphan Society's Charity Bachelor Auction was about to get under way, and it appeared that every single woman in Boston was here to bid on a dream date.

"Oh, Lord," Con muttered under her breath, "this is going to be a long night."

She bought a drink at one of the four bars set up around the ballroom and found her way to a reserved table near the front. One of the perks of being the society editor at the *Courier* was being able to snag the best seat in the house. A stage had been set up, the place where the twenty hunkiest men in Boston were soon to be auctioned off to the highest bidders.

"Talk about your meat markets," an excruciatingly thin woman said from across the table when Connie took her seat. "Doesn't this just take the cake?"

Connie smiled and turned to inspect the men on stage. There were twenty of them, but only one interested Connie. She searched the stage for Bachelor Number 12. She smiled to herself when she spied him. Tall, broad-shouldered and commanding, Jed Duval looked uncomfortable with the entire proceedings. Hunching his muscular shoulders beneath his tux, he ran a blunt finger around his shirt collar.

Connie smiled. He looked about as comfortable as a bull at a tea party, but before the night was over, he'd be even more uncomfortable. She'd deposited one thousand dollars in her checking account for this evening, and when she went home, she'd go with the assurance that Jed Duval would be hers for an entire weekend.

When the auction started, Connie sat back and enjoyed the show.

Down went the first, four bachelors, then the next four, then three more. She watched these paragons of male virtue and didn't feel even a hint of attraction for them. Only when Bachelor Number 12 strolled toward the podium did Connie sit up.

"And now, ladies," the emcee intoned, "Bachelor Number 12. He's the winningest pitcher in baseball and the pride of our own Barons...." Loud cheers erupted in the ballroom. "And he'll whisk you off to a private island off the coast of Maine for a carefree weekend that he says will allow you to get back to nature and enjoy the simple pleasures of life." The emcee leered at the audience. "And we all wonder just what Bachelor Number 12 means by that, don't we, ladies?"

The appreciative audience whooped and hollered, and Connie saw Duval's discomfort at being the object of such undisguised female admiration. Connie glanced around uneasily. Jed Duval was proving more popular than any of the other bachelors who'd gone before him. She just might have competition.

For the first time, she allowed herself to see Jed Duval as simply a man, not the object of her unrelenting desire to get a story. For all his rough-hewn toughness, he was undeniably attractive. His skin was dark, his eyes were an almost unnatural gray, surrounded by lines from squinting in the sun, and his dark hair was slightly shaggy, which only seemed to add to the aura that surrounded him. There was a magnetism about him; he exuded an earthy virility, something missing in the other men with their immaculately fitted tuxedos and cosmopolitan manners.

Connie shifted in her chair, dismayed by the idea of being alone with him for two nights, unsupervised. In the clubhouse last week, there had been undeniable sexual sparks between the two of them. Maybe she was biting off more than she could chew.

She snorted to herself contemptuously. She had to remember why she was doing this. It certainly wasn't for romance. She'd put up with two days with Jed Duval if she got what she wanted in the end. She put aside the disturbing thought that Duval might subject her to something she hadn't planned on and concentrated on the stage.

"And now, ladies," the emcee shouted into the microphone, "let's open the bidding for Bachelor Number 12, Jed Duval!"

"One thousand dollars!" one woman shouted from the back.

"One thousand five hundred!" shouted another.

"Two thousand!"

"Two thousand two hundred fifty!"

Connie felt her throat close up. So far, the highest bid had been for a CEO of a major electronics firm, and he'd only gone for a little over a thousand dollars. The thousand dollars she'd been given by Vinnie Carbone was useless. For a minute a feeling of panic swept over her, then she swallowed uncomfortably and raised a determined hand. "Two thousand five hundred," she said. She had a seven-thousand-dollar credit line on her Master Card, and tonight it was going to get used.

There was a momentary pause after she bid, then the room erupted in shouts. "Three thousand!" screamed the frenzied woman in the back.

"Three thousand two hundred-fifty," shouted another.

Connie lifted her chin. "Four thousand," she said clearly.

A hush fell over the room. The emcee looked around the audience. "We have a bid of four thousand dollars for Bachelor Number 12. It's safe to say that bidding for Mr. Duval has set new records for our charity event. Do I hear four thousand two fifty?"

There was an expectant rustle in the room, then the woman from the back of the room shouted, "Four thousand two-fifty!" Squeals of delight mingled with exuberant applause, but Connie quieted things with a gesture of her hand. "Five thousand dollars," she said. If Vinnie Carbone didn't agree to reimburse her, this interview might send her to the poorhouse.

A unified gasp floated through the ballroom but Connie didn't pay it any mind. She was staring at Duval. He leaned against the podium, resting his bulk on one elbow as he gazed at her with steel gray eyes. For a moment she wondered if she was doing the right thing, then she dismissed her doubts. She wasn't doing this for herself, she had to remember, but for the paper. She had a job to do, and she was going to do it.

"Going...going...gone!" the emcee shouted. Exuberantly, he banged the gavel on the podium. "Five thousand dollars for Jed Duval!"

Applause thundered in the room. Laughter and conversation crackled with excitement. Waiters rushed to fill orders before the next bidding could begin, but Connie ignored it all. She took out her Master Card with a trembling hand. She might look unrattled, but inside she was a wreck.

"You must have wanted that date with Mr. Duval real bad," said the girl who came to her table to write up her sales receipt.

Connie smiled, but decided to ignore the comment.

"Would you ask Mr. Duval to meet me in the cocktail lounge, please?" she asked. She rose and walked out of the crowded room, oblivious to the awed stares and whispers that followed her as she left.

Shaking, she made her way to the elevator and collapsed against its wall. It seemed to take forever to travel down twenty-four stories to the cocktail lounge on the street level, but she didn't mind. She wasn't ready to face Jed Duval just yet. Maybe with a stiff drink in her hand, she'd feel better.

"CONSTANCE KENYON," a deep male voice said from behind her. "Still after a story. She's so hungry she'll buy one, if she has to."

Connie swiveled slowly on the bar stool and found herself face-to-face with Jed Duval.

"Hello, Duval," she said softly.

"You're one mighty determined woman, aren't you, Ms. Kenyon?" he asked, taking a seat next to her at the bar.

When his muscular thigh brushed hers, she raised a cool eyebrow. She was determined to act as if nothing bothered her. She hoped that would drive Duval crazy. For some reason, she wanted to rankle him. Something about his cool disdain made her want to shake him up.

Duval took out a slender cheroot. "Smoke?"

"I don't smoke."

"Naw," Duval said, grinning as he lit the thin cigar. "I don't believe it. For some reason, the thought of vice and you go together."

"Sorry to disappoint you," she said, smiling coolly. "Appearances can be deceiving."

Duval silently harrumphed.

"Look, Duval," she said, "I know you're annoyed with me—"

"Annoyed?" he said, examining his cigar intently. He let the cold bottle of beer sit untouched on the bar in front of him. "No, Ms. Kenyon, I'm not annoyed. That's too mild a word. Angry might be better. Or maybe I'm completely furious, but annoyed?" He shook his head and clamped the cigar between his teeth. "Annoyed just doesn't do it justice, Con."

"You don't have an understanding bone in your body, do you, Duval?" she asked, turning her blue eyes on him.

"Oh, I understand you, Con. I understand you real well. You're ambitious. You want the story that no other reporter has been able to get, all for the greater glory and good of one Constance Kenyon, two-bit society editor."

She shivered. He had a way of making ambition sound ugly, as if it were something she should be ashamed of. "I'm not like the others, Jed—"

"No?" he asked, chortling. "Is that how you explain your job to yourself at night so you can sleep?" His gray eyes were filled with contempt. "Come on, Kenyon. Stop kidding yourself. You want to make a name for yourself and you want it now, without the hard work and the sweat—"

"I work hard!" she said, her voice throbbing with anger. "You don't think hanging out in a lousy locker room isn't hard on me? You think I wouldn't rather be over at the Ritz, covering a tea party?"

"Frankly, no. If you wanted to be covering tea parties, you would be. No, Con, you're just like all the others. You want to ride me to fame like a flea rides a dog. Without the promise of a big story on me, you'd still be stuck doing the gossip column. Well, get used to it, Con, because you won't get a story out of me. Not now, not ever."

"You think you'll be able to spend two days with me on a deserted island without talking, Duval?"

"You bet I will, honey. Every time I look at you I'll see blazing headlines instead of a good-looking woman. That'll keep me from talking."

"What have you got to hide, Duval?" she asked in a low voice, her eyes narrowed as she studied his face.

He laughed scornfully. "I'm not hiding anything."

"Oh, come on," she said. "You think I buy that? You're hiding something. It may take a while to come out, but it will, and when it does, you'll be glad it's me who's writing the story and not some writer without scruples or a heart."

"Scruples!" He laughed out loud. "Oh, come on, Con, you're killing me. You've got about as many scruples as a rat in an alley. And as for heart . . ." He laughed again, scorn echoing in his low voice. "Your heart is about as soft as a lizard's hide, Constance Kenyon. Believe me, if it ever comes to a test of whose interests come first, I won't stand a chance."

She studied his face, seeing bitterness in his disillusioned eyes. Somebody had hurt this man badly. She felt a pang in that heart he'd said was as tough as a lizard's hide. For a moment she wished she could forget about the story, forget about fame and ambition and the need to prove herself, and just reach out and take his hand. He needed someone to soothe his wounds, not add to them, but she realized that wasn't her job. Wasn't that what Vinnie Carbone had said? She wasn't a social worker; she was a reporter.

"I wish it didn't have to be like this between us," she said quietly.

"Oh, sure, Con," he said bitterly. "What are you hoping? That I'll turn to you for comfort?" He gazed at her with jaded eyes. "That'd be like turning to a rattler for snake-bite remedy."

"You won't believe me, will you?" she said, her voice soft as she looked into his eyes. "You won't let yourself believe me. In your own way, you're as determined as I am, Duval, only you're determined to hold me out."

"Don't try to sweet-talk me, Con. It won't work."

"Because you won't let it," she said. "You've made up your mind about me and nothing's going to change it. I could walk on hot coals and you'd still see me as a scheming reporter, out to get glory at the expense of your hide."

"Aren't you?"

She stared into his eyes, then let out a defeated sigh. "Yes, I am."

He stared at her, the surprise at her answer evident in his face. "Well, what do you know? Con's gotten smart. She's decided to try the honest approach."

She laughed to herself, shaking her head as she looked into space. "I admit it. I want this story. It will be a big boost to my career, but I'm not going to sell my soul to get it."

"Well, at least you admit your real reasons for wanting the story on me."

"Hey, what can I say," she said, shrugging. "I've got reporting in my blood." She eyed him speculatively. "I can't help but wonder about you. I look at this man who's on the top of the heap but won't talk about it and I wonder—what's this guy really like? What makes him tick?" She smiled knowingly. "I just want to know, and when you tell me I can't know, it makes me even more determined that I will. So here we are, Duval, just you and me, pitted against each other."

"Sort of a power struggle, eh, Kenyon?"

"Kind of."

"So who you think's going to win?"

She eyed him ironically. "You see? You've got this mind-set—that one of us is going to win and the other lose. I don't see it that way, Duval. I see both of us winning."

"Interesting how a person can justify her behavior," he said, grinning sardonically.

"I'm not rationalizing, Duval."

"No?" He studied her with withering eyes. "Don't bet on it, Con."

She sighed and pushed money toward the bartender. "The drinks are on me, Duval."

He pushed her money away. "The day I let a reporter pay for my drinks, I'll quit baseball."

She hunched her shoulders as if to ward off his contempt. "Look, let's just get the particulars down, okay? I need to know where to meet you Friday, that kind of thing."

"I pitch Thursday night," he said. "I'll probably sleep late Friday morning. I'll pick you up in front of the *Courier* Friday afternoon about one. We'll take off for Maine and get to Port Jade in about four hours."

"Then what?"

"We'll take the ferry over to the island."

"So we'll be there Friday night?"

"That's right." His eyes traveled down her scornfully. "You better bring a couple pairs of jeans and a warm jacket. I've got running water, but that's about it. It's rustic, Con, not the kind of fancy place a woman like you is used to."

"Sounds delightful," she said sarcastically. So he thought she was used to fancy places, did he? Then the laugh was on him.

"Hey, you wanted to come along," he said, grinning as if he liked the idea of her being uncomfortable. "Should be a new experience for a society dame." He eyed her knowingly. "I suppose that's what your story will be about—'Roughing it with Jed Duval.'"

"That's the kind of thing a society editor would write."

"Which is exactly what you are," he pointed out.

"But not what I want to be." Her eyes were cool as she studied him. "No, Duval, I want a real story."

He studied her with narrowed eyes. "Why, Con?" His voice was low, almost caressing. His eyes seemed to smoulder. An almost sexual tension crackled in the air between them. "You've got a ready-made story. Why won't you write it?"

"Because I told you I'd never write anything about you without your approval. I meant it, Duval. You may think I'm so ambitious I'd cut my own mother's throat, but I'm not. Honor means something to me. More than anything, I want your trust."

A hint of a smile played around his lips. "Tell me another one, Con," he murmured. "Come on, try to really convince me. Wind me around that pretty little finger of yours."

She got down off the bar stool. "Think what you want, Duval. See you Friday at one." She turned and walked out of the lounge, leaving Jed Duval staring thoughtfully after her, his bottle of beer still untouched.

Chapter Five

On Thursday night, Jed Duval lost his first major-league game. It stunned passionate fans, silenced the network television commentators, quieted for a moment even the radio broadcasters. Gloom seemed to settle over Boston as the fans sat in their seats, watching Jed Duval get shellacked by an aggressive San Francisco Giants team.

Con sat in front of her television, staring at Jed's bleak face as he tried to pitch himself out of trouble, praying for him to regain his control, begging him silently.

"Come on, Jed," she urged, her hands squeezed into impotent fists. "Come on."

Nothing worked. He gave up two successive singles, a double, another single, and then a home run that cleared the bases. To make matters worse, he was called for a wild pitch.

When Shorty Summers, the manager of the Barons, walked out to the mound, he didn't even look at Duval. He merely signaled the bull pen for a right-hander, and Jed turned and walked off the mound.

The Boston Barons fans rose as one in their seats and gave him an astounding rafter-raising ovation. With his head bent, he went into the dugout, but the fans kept clapping. They stood in the stands under the bright lights of Barons Field and refused to stop until at last Jed Duval came up the dugout steps and took off his hat to the fans.

And then the applause exploded, and the noise and cheering crescendoed and the young boys in the stands were crying, and their fathers and uncles had tears in their eyes and contorted faces, and the women cried openly, tears streaming down their faces, as they all seemed to realize, perhaps only subliminally, that they had just witnessed the work of a man who had become a hero.

Watching television, Connie cried, tears streaming down her face, her heart bursting inside her, filling her with pride and reverence for what he had accomplished. As the cameras zoomed in on Jed's face, she felt her heart rise up inside her.

It was such a public forum, she thought, staring at his emotionless face. He had stood on a ball field on the outskirts of Boston and the public spotlight had shone on him in an unrelenting way, had watched his every move, analyzed every pitch, commented on his style, his mannerisms, his amazing trip from oblivion in the minor leagues to the zenith of stardom in the major leagues, and tonight, in front of thousands of fans at Barons Field and millions of television viewers nationwide, it had all come to an end.

When most people failed, Con realized, they did so in the privacy of their offices and homes, unbothered by the gaze and expectations of a nation. When a major-league ball player failed, he did so in front of the nation.

She watched through her tears as Jed stood and accepted the adulation of his fans, his face stalwart, unflinching. She shivered as goose bumps traveled up and down her arms. Tonight, she knew, she had witnessed greatness.

She watched till the bitter end. The Barons lost 11 to 3. Jed Duval's major-league pitching record stood at 29 and 1.

When she turned off the television, she was exhausted. She took a shower and fell into bed, but she couldn't sleep. She lay and stared up at the shadows that played across her ceiling, saw the lace curtain at her window lift and fall in the soft night breeze, heard the sound of a car honking in the distance, a dog barking, heard someone arguing in an apartment across the street.

She turned on her side and stared into the darkness. Tomorrow she would see him. It was an extraordinary opportunity, yet she found herself not wanting to meet him, trying to think of any excuse to put off their weekend trip. She suddenly didn't want to be such an intimate witness to Jed Duval's defeat. She didn't want to see his face, look into his eyes, didn't want to hear his voice. With the instincts of a lover, she wanted to leave him alone, give him time and space.

She laughed at herself. Ironic, wasn't it? She stared into the darkness and wished tomorrow would never come.

SE STOOD OUTSIDE the offices of the *Boston Courier*, a suitcase at her feet, turning her head right and left, peering at the sluggish traffic, wondering which direction he'd come from, what kind of car he'd drive. She didn't want to think about what she'd say to him.

"Sorry about the game, Jed."

She grimaced to herself. What could she say that wasn't useless, silly, demeaning to his pride?

She glanced at her watch and began to get nervous. He was late. This wasn't like Jed Duval, who showed up early for every game, like clockwork, the coaches had assured her. "Jed Duval is never late."

Then again, Jed Duval never talked to reporters either.

She swallowed her fear and told herself to calm down. He'd be here. He wouldn't fink out on her. He'd promised the Orphan Society to participate in the auction, and they wouldn't get to keep the sizable sum she'd bid if he failed to deliver on his promise. It was all there in the fine print on the bottom of the contract she'd signed.

She shifted her knapsack from one shoulder to the other and peered at a Blazer that pulled up in front of the steps of the *Courier*'s impressive rococo entrance. She stepped away from the gargoyle she'd been leaning against and peered into the vehicle.

It was Duval. He shifted the truck into park and got out. "Ms. Kenyon," he said, nodding formally as he stooped to pick up her suitcase.

She didn't say anything, just got in the truck and fastened her seat belt.

When he got in, she met his eyes. "I'm sorry about the game, Duval."

"Had to happen sometime." He threw the Blazer into first and glided into the slow-moving downtown traffic.

She stared at him, rattled by his composure. Here she'd been dreading having to be with him the day after his national defeat and he was acting like it didn't even matter. "Well, I must say, you're taking it well."

"I got a lot of practice losing in the minors. It doesn't feel much different now that I'm in the major leagues."

She had to admire the way he handled the situation. If it had been she, she'd have been bawling in a beer somewhere, feeling sorry for herself that her winning streak had come to an end. She took out a pad of paper and wrote down his words.

Immediately, Duval stiffened. Raising her head, she glanced at him. "This must be hard on you," she said softly.

He shook his head, his face set, closed up. "I'm sorry, but I don't have anything to say."

She sighed and put her pad and pen in her pocketbook. "Okay," she said, "you win. No notes, no tape recorders. Just you and me."

"Eureka," he said sarcastically, and gunned the engine to slide onto the highway that headed toward Maine.

They drove in silence for an hour, he with both hands on the wheel and his eyes on the road, she nestled into the corner between the door and her seat, watching him as he drove.

"You learning anything?" he finally asked when they'd passed the Maine border and were headed toward Portland.

"That you're a truly stubborn man," she said, smiling softly.

He glanced at her, then looked back at the road. "You already knew that."

She sighed. "Yes."

He took a pack of cigarettes out and shook one out, then held the pack out to her. "Smoke?"

"I told you the other night, Duval. I don't smoke."

He held the cigarette lighter to the end of the cigarette and puffed until it was lit. "So you did." He replaced the lighter and glanced at her. "Mind if I do?"

She shrugged. "It's your life."

"That's big of you," he said, his voice edged with bitterness.

"Look, Duval," she said. "Why don't you make the best of it? You're stuck with me for the next two days. I won't go away and you can't get away. Let's forget the past and start over, okay? Let's pretend we're friends."

He grunted humorlessly and flicked her an almost amused look. "You wish, Kenyon."

"Yes," she said slowly, "I do."

He glanced at her, as if surprised. "Yeah?"

She studied his profile when he turned back to the road. "I cried last night," she said softly. "I was watching the game on TV. It was an incredible moment, Duval. They'll be talking about your winning streak fifty years from now."

His face was set, tough, emotionless. He stared straight ahead. "It's a game, Kenyon. Don't try to make it more than it is."

She felt angry at his stubbornness, at his damnable refusal to accept her praise, but she held her temper. "You know that's not true, Duval," she said. "What you did is special."

He twisted his neck, rubbing it with his large callused hand. "Don't try to wangle your way into favor with praise, Kenyon. I never liked apple polishers."

"I'm not apple polishing!"

He grunted. "Ha."

She threw him an angry look and straightened in her seat, turning to face straight ahead. "You're not stubborn, Duval, you're simply thick."

His face grew ruddy, as if her words had somehow struck him. He stabbed her with his eyes. "Ball players can't all be as smart as hotshot reporters."

"Most manage to be," she shot back.

He gripped the steering wheel so hard his knuckles turned white. "I suppose you're a college graduate," he said in a tight voice. "One of those smart girls who always made honor roll and graduated first in her class."

"What's it to you?" she snapped. "You were probably a dumb jock."

"I'm not talking to you anymore, Kenyon," he muttered. "We don't have one damn thing in common."

"We could have, if you'd stop assuming I'm out to get you."

"What do you expect me to think? There were twenty-five reporters milling around outside my apartment this afternoon, and a half dozen photographers. That's why I was late. They're like flies around a carcass."

"If you want to know the truth," she retorted, "I didn't even want to come with you this weekend. I thought you might want some time alone. I'm not heartless, Duval, and my hide's not made out of alligator."

"Bull," he said succinctly.

She glared at him. "You look for trouble, you know that, Duval? You expect it. You're so bitter, you can't believe any one could care about you."

"Care about me?" he whooped. "I see, now you're latching onto the female angle." He glanced at her knowingly. "I might have expected it. Charlie Huff warned me about you."

"And you believe Charlie Huff?" she cried. "Why? He's just another reporter, Duval. Why would you trust him any more than you trust me?"

"At least he makes his living off baseball. He's not after me just for a hot story."

She sighed in exasperation and turned her head to look out the window. "You're hopeless."

"Then leave me alone."

"Fine. I won't say another word the entire weekend."

"That's the kind of thing dreams are made of," he said sarcastically.

She gave him a dirty look and settled back in her seat. It was going to be a long weekend.

Chapter Six

Port Jade turned out to be a harbor town a couple hours north of Portland. There was a gas station, a café, a general store and a row of shabby warehouses at a fishing dock, where three dilapidated fishing boats bobbed peacefully on the water. Nearby, an old man with a bushy gray beard worked on some lobster traps. He wore dirty brown pants and a grimy undershirt that had long since turned gray. On his head was a navy blue wool knitted seaman's cap.

Connie pointed to a hand-lettered sign that was tacked up on a post. "Ferry closed," it read. "Come back tomorrow."

"Great," she said, "looks like we're out of luck. What do we do now?"

"I don't know," he said, rubbing a hand on his pant leg.

"Well, we can't just sit here," she said. "Maybe that old guy knows what's going on."

Jed's eyes darted to the old man who continued working on the lobster traps. "You wait here," he said, opening the door.

"Over my dead body," she said, and scrambled out beside him.

"Excuse me," Jed said to the old man. "I have to get to Jade Island."

The old man didn't look up. "Ferry's closed today."

"Well, can't someone else take us out to the island?" he asked.

"If they could," the old man snapped, "they would. Art'll be back tomorrow. Come back then."

"Great," Jed said under his breath. He stood with his hands in his back pockets, staring out at the island that was just visible on the horizon.

"Honestly, Jed," Connie said irritably, "if I didn't know better, I'd swear you set this up to get out of spending the weekend with me."

He turned to look at her with angry eyes. "I gave you my word, Con. This is as much of a surprise to me as it is to you."

"Well, fine, then what are we going to do? Camp here overnight?"

Jed looked at the boats. "One of these yours?" he asked the old man.

"Nope," he answered.

"You know who owns them?" Jed asked.

"Yep."

Jed stood with his hands on his lean hips, staring down at the man as he worked on the lobster trap. Getting information out of a Maine native was a lot like fishing in an unstocked pond. "Can you tell me where the boat owners might be?"

"Might be anywhere," the old man said. He raised his head and looked at Jed through squinty eyes. "You sure do look familiar. You from around here?"

"No," Jed said. Turning, he walked toward the Blazer.

Connie fell into step beside him. "I thought you had everything arranged, Duval," she said with soft irony.

"I thought I did, too," he said, slamming the door and starting the engine.

"You're a man of few words, Duval."

"Comes from being around people from Maine," he said, putting the Blazer in gear and heading toward the general store.

"Are you from Maine?"

"Nope."

While this might not be the most auspicious time to probe his origins, she decided to try. "The Barons bio says you were born in Waco, Texas."

"If you knew that, why'd you ask if I'm from Maine?"

"Did you grow up in Waco?" she asked, ignoring his question.

"Nope."

"Where'd you grow up?"

"All over."

"That a place in Texas?"

He chuckled softly. "No."

"Well, you had to have lived somewhere," she said, refusing to give up.

"We didn't stay in one place very long."

"We?"

"My dad and me."

Now she was getting somewhere. "You didn't have any brothers or sisters?"

"No."

"What about your mother?"

He pulled up in front of the store and cut the engine. "She died when I was born." He got out and slammed the door before she could say anything. Scrambling out of the Blazer, Connie caught up with him at the top of the steps.

"So it was just you and your Dad?" she asked.

"That's right," he said, holding the door open for her. They entered a store that could have existed fifty years earlier. Shelves were piled high with every thing imaginable.

A blue-haired woman with a wrinkled face, wearing a misbuttoned gray cardigan sweater, stood behind the counter. "H'lo," she said sourly. "What can I do for you?"

"I need someone to take me out to Jade Island," Jed said.

"Art Baker runs the ferry," the old woman said. "Runs twice a day—ten in the morning and four in the afternoon."

"Not today," Jed said. "Ferry's closed."

"Well," the old woman said, shrugging, "looks like you're out of luck." She turned away and went back to reading the paper.

"Helpful type, isn't she?" Connie asked under her breath.

Jed cleared his throat. The woman lowered the newspaper. "Is there anyone who could take us out there?" he asked.

"Nope."

Jed sighed, his eyes on the inflatable dory that hung suspended from the rafters overhead. "I suppose I could buy a boat..."

"Oh, no, you don't," Connie said, speaking up. "I'm not letting you take me out in the Atlantic Ocean in a rubber boat!"

"Great. Then what do you propose we do tonight? Camp out on the dock?"

"There must be a motel somewhere around here," Connie said, looking toward the old woman.

"Port Jade Inn's a couple miles out of town," she said. "They might have a room."

"Fine," Connie said. "We'll stay there." Turning, she walked out of the store.

"This wasn't part of the deal, Kenyon," Jed said as they drove up Route 1 looking for the Port Jade Inn.

"Neither was Art's not being here," she replied airily. "But that's all right, Duval, I won't hold it against you. We're still spending the weekend together. It's just not the weekend you planned."

"I could have bought a boat," he grumbled.

"Over my dead body," she said, then spied the neatly painted sign. "There it is." She broke into a smile when she saw the inn. "Why, it's nice!"

It was a gracious, old Victorian house with white-painted clapboards and shiny green shutters. A porch ran along the front and sides, where white wicker rockers and couches sat about in open invitation. Window boxes bloomed with geraniums and petunias and the ocean dashed upon the rocks directly across the street, sending plumes of salt spray fifty feet into the air.

Jed stared at the six or seven cars sitting in the parking lot. "Look, we could still go back to Boston. We could do this some other time."

"No backing out, Duval," Connie said, laughing as she opened the door of the Blazer. "Come on, let's at least see if they have a room."

"A room?" he repeated.

"Oh." Her face skittered away from his and she felt pink color creep into her face. "Look, I'll pay for my own room."

"What if they don't have two rooms?" he asked.

"Oh, come on, Jed, stop making excuses. They probably have lots of empty rooms. This is only early June. It's not vacation season yet."

"SORRY," THE CLERK said, looking from Jed to Connie, "we've only got one room left. A single with twin beds and a private bath."

She glanced at Jed, who gave her an "I told you so" look. "You don't have any other rooms available?" she asked.

"Sorry, ma'am, just this one room. There's an antique show going on this weekend and people are here from all over. Every inn and bed-and-breakfast I know of are filled to the gills. You'd have to go back to Portland to find a room tonight."

"I see." Connie glanced at Jed. "Could I talk to you in private?"

He followed her outside to the porch. "Okay," she said. "So what do we do now?"

"We either go back to Portland or take the only room they've got," Jed said grimly. "Believe me, it's not how I imagined this weekend starting out."

"No," she said sharply, "you probably envisioned drowning me when you got me in the damn boat."

"Look, things happen," Jed said. "Let's just take the room and be done with it."

Connie stared at the ocean that crashed onto the rocky shore. She and Jed were adults—she supposed they could handle sharing a room. At least it had twin beds. But something made her hesitate, some vestige perhaps of her long forgotten Catholic upbringing. "All right," she said at last. "Just don't get any ideas, Duval. You make one move toward me tonight and I'll bean you with a fireplace poker."

The corner of Jed's mouth lifted humorously. "If you're afraid to share a room in an inn with me, I can hardly wait to see how you'll react to being on an island alone with me."

She gave him a knowing look. "It'd make a great story, Duval—'Pitcher Killed by Woman Defending Her Honor.'" Turning, she stalked into the lobby, the sound of Jed's chuckle ringing in her ears.

The clerk handed Jed a pen and a small three-by-five index card. "If you'll just fill this in, I'll get your bags out of your car and bring them up to your room."

Connie leaned over to whisper in his ear. "Just sign in as Mr. and Mrs. Duval."

He looked at her and nodded, then scribbled something indecipherable on the card.

The clerk handed him the key to Room 12. "It's just up these stairs and all the way down the hall to the right. I'll just go out and get your bags and bring them right up for you."

Jed took Connie by the elbow. "Well," he said, guiding her up the stairs, "this is going to make one helluva story, Miss Big-time Reporter."

She didn't bother to reply. They found Room 12 at the end of the hall. He fit the key in the door and opened it to reveal a small corner room with twin beds. There were two windows, one overlooking the backyard where flowers bloomed in profusion. The side window allowed them a glimpse of the ocean. The two beds were separated by a nightstand containing a lamp and a black rotary-dial telephone. There was an overstuffed wing chair upholstered in a faded pink floral print in the corner and an old-fashioned white painted dresser. There was no television, but a bookcase held dozens of old books.

"At least we have something to read," Connie said when Jed closed the door behind them.

Jed grunted, then opened a window and leaned on the sill. "We should have gone back to Boston," he said testily.

"Let's try to make the best of it, Duval," Connie said. "The ferry will be running tomorrow. We just have to get through the night without killing each other."

"That might be easier said than done," he said, straightening from the window.

She swallowed uncomfortably. The room suddenly seemed awfully small. There was barely room for the two of them. She shrugged off the thought and tried to look unconcerned. "We're adults, Duval. We can manage to be civil."

He gave her a sour look and elbowed his way past her toward the bathroom. "Just keep your distance," he said. "I'm used to living alone."

"So am I," she retorted. "You think I like this any better than you do?"

"Well, you paid enough for the privilege of spending the weekend with me."

"All in the line of duty, Duval. Don't get any misconceptions. This is business, not pleasure."

His eyes slid over her body. "Maybe we should do something about that," he said softly.

She felt chills feather over her skin. Backing up, she came up against the bed. A sudden picture of him and her on the bed, locked in passionate lovemaking, came to her. She felt her cheeks turn pink, felt herself begin to tremble with awareness of him. She tried to look anywhere but at him, yet her eyes seemed glued to his face. She could see him staring at her, a slight smile on his face, as if he realized what she was thinking.

"Don't even think about it, Duval," she said quietly.

He smiled. "Thinking won't hurt any."

"It will if it gives you ideas."

"I've had ideas since the first time I saw you," he said, leaning back against the wall and crossing his arms. "But don't worry, Con, I won't act on them." He cocked his head and grinned. "Unless you insist on it."

A knock on the door made her jump. "Forget it," she said, and went to the door.

The desk clerk stood in the hall, their suitcases in his hands. He deposited them on the beds and pocketed a generous tip. As he closed the door on his way out, he suddenly stopped. "I almost forgot," he said, handing Con a small white card, "your husband didn't complete the registration card. You can drop it down later."

"My husband? Oh, yes." Smiling, Con saw him out and brought the card to Jed. "Husband, you forgot to fill this out."

"And I'm not going to," he said in a gruff voice. He shoved it back toward her. "I'm going to get something in the car. You do it."

Con was taken aback by his harshness and bristled. "How am I supposed to do this?" she shot back. "I don't even know your license-plate number."

"PITCHR," he said and bolted from the room, leaving Con aghast.

She looked down at the card and shook her head. Who did he think he was to boss her around? Maybe this playacting was going to his head, she thought. He was beginning to act like a real husband!

Chapter Seven

She was seated in the dining room a few hours later, nursing a drink, when Jed appeared. He took a seat across from her and ordered a beer.

"Why didn't you tell me why you didn't want to fill the card in, Jed?" Connie asked.

He seemed to stiffen. "What do you mean?"

"Look," she said, "I can understand your wanting to keep your address and phone number private. When I realized that, I filled in my address and phone number. That should keep your privacy intact."

She could see him relax as she spoke. "Thanks," he said. "I appreciate your understanding."

"But you didn't have to be so rude about it, you know."

"I'm sorry."

She shook off his words. "It must be hard, being a hero."

He grunted. "I'm no hero, Connie."

"But you are, whether you want to be or not."

He stared at his beer bottle, scraping off the label with his thumb. "I never bargained on anything that's happened to me," he said quietly. "All I ever wanted to do was pitch in the big leagues. I guess I didn't think about what could happen once I got here."

"Do you have any regrets?" she asked softly.

He shrugged. "Some, I suppose, but not about baseball. I'm doing what I love, the only thing I know how to do. Baseball's my life. I wouldn't know what to do if I couldn't throw a ball."

"But you must have thought about it all those years while you were playing in the minors. I mean, from what I understand, most people don't last that long in the minors, much less get to the majors after ten years."

He smiled, still scraping the label off his beer. "I always believed I could do it," he said. "I just had to come a long way. I had to unlearn a lot of bad habits, then learn all new good habits. It took me a lot longer than it does most guys."

"Yeah, I guess most guys play in Little League and on high school teams, that sort of thing."

He raised his eyes to hers. "We moved a lot," he said quietly. "I didn't stay in one town long enough to be on a team."

"It must have been rough," she said softly.

He shrugged, taking a swig of beer. "I managed."

"I can understand and respect you for not asking for pity, Jed," Connie said softly, "but you could cut yourself a little slack. It wouldn't hurt to admit that things were rough when you were a kid."

"When you're growing up, all you know is the life you have. It becomes normal. I didn't think of it as being hard. The point is, I did manage, and I'm none the worse for any of it. I don't ask for sympathy, because I don't need it."

"I wasn't talking about sympathy, Jed. You're right, you don't need any. You're an amazing man. But I believe that forces shape our lives and make us what we are. Things that happen to us in childhood reverberate through the rest of our lives. I guess I'm wondering what happened to you as a child to make you the way you are now."

"Is that the reporter or the woman wondering?" he asked.

She smiled. "Both. You can't separate one from the other."

"I think you can," he said. "Everyone leaves their jobs behind some time. I know I do."

"Maybe it's easier for you to do that," she said. "For me, I'm always thinking, questioning, wondering about people. That's what makes me a reporter. I'm insatiably curious." She smiled lopsidedly. "I have to admit, though, it does get tiring at times. Sometimes I wish I could just stop questioning and relax, but I don't seem to be able to."

"What happened in your childhood to make you the way you are?"

She stared at her drink, then rubbed her eyes. "Let's just say my childhood wasn't the stuff dreams are made of."

"Oh, come on, Con, you look like you had the best life in the world—a nice house in the suburbs, parents who loved you, good schools . . ."

She smiled wryly. "Things are seldom the way they appear, Duval."

"Ain't that the truth?"

The waitress approached and handed them menus. "I'll be back to take your orders in a minute."

Connie smiled and looked over the menu. Jed kept his closed in front of him. When the waitress arrived to take their orders, he ordered steak.

"Sorry," the waitress said. "We have filet mignon and prime rib, but no steak."

"I'll have the filet," he said.

Connie frowned, watching him from beneath her lashes. He looked as if he wanted to bolt from the table and never come back. He was gripping the menu as if his life depended on it, nodding at the waitress who was telling him he could have either green beans or broccoli.

Lifting her eyes, she stared at Duval, realizing slowly how nervous he was. This sudden insight affected her more than anything she'd found out about him in the past month. Here was a man who was completely unschooled in the so-called social graces, a big, strong hunk of a man who was utterly miserable away from the baseball park. There he was in complete control, the master of his game. Here, away from all he knew and felt comfortable with, he was shy, insecure, even awkward, like a young schoolboy on a field trip to Europe.

She felt something deep inside herself open up to him, felt her own guard go down as understanding flowered within her. "Relax, Jed," she said softly when the waitress had gone. "Don't be so nervous."

"Who's nervous?" he snapped.

She met his gaze with quietly amused eyes. He looked down and for a minute she thought he was going to get up and walk away. He just swallowed and looked up at her. "I guess I am a little nervous at that," he admitted.

"You still don't trust me, do you?" Connie said. "Look, I promised you I wouldn't write any story without your approval, and I meant it. Just forget who I am."

His eyes darkened. "That could be dangerous."

She felt chills run up and down her arms. She couldn't look away, couldn't break the electric current that suddenly seemed to permeate the air around them. She felt her breathing grow shallow, felt her heart begin to pump harder. A sweet yearning rose inside her, a kind of distant voice crying out for her attention.

"He's a man," it said. *"Forget the story. Forget work. Forget everything but him."*

She shivered and broke eye contact, looking down at the table, trembling inside, feeling suddenly uncertain, vulnerable. She wondered if one room would be big enough for the two of them, even if there were twin beds.

"This could get to be complicated."

"It already is complicated, Con," Jed said softly. "You just didn't realize it till now."

She took a steadying breath. "Look, I've got a story to write. Let's not forget who and what I am, okay?"

"Answer me one question, Con. What's the real reason you've been bugging me? Isn't this story just an excuse?"

"An excuse?" She stared at him blankly. "An excuse for what?"

"Maybe you went to that bachelor auction because you really want a man in your life."

She burst out laughing, but even to her own ears it sounded much too nervous. "You've got to be joking!"

He stared at her with disconcertingly direct gray eyes. "Then why me, Con? Why not Roger Clemens or Wade Boggs? What've I got they don't have?"

"A past," she replied, forcing herself to meet his gaze directly. "You're a blank sheet of paper, Jed. All those others you mentioned are open books. You're not. Why, Jed? What are you afraid of?"

He lowered his eyes so they were shielded by his lashes. A muscle worked rhythmically in his cheek. He was suddenly quiet, alert, as if he were a jungle animal sensing danger. She almost shivered at his sudden shift of mood.

"I've seen guys destroyed by the hype, Con, eaten up and spat out for all the world to see. I don't want that. I'm not comfortable in the public eye. I just want to do my job and be left alone."

"You're very naive, Jed," she said softly. "The world's not going to leave you alone. It's going to keep knocking on your door till you answer. By not talking to reporters, you're almost assuring that we'll keep bugging you. You've become a kind of mission for some of us."

"Fine," he said shortly. "Then do the damn article you want so bad. Write about spending a weekend with a famous baseball player. Get it out of your system, Con, then leave me alone."

There. She had it. He had finally given his permission to write a story about him, but she didn't feel a sense of victory. If anything, she felt deflated, let down, like a child who finally opened her Christmas stocking only to find oranges and nuts instead of a longed-for toy.

What had she expected to feel when she finally wore him down? Elation? A sense of winning a hard-fought game? She pushed her fork around the table, trying to figure out what she was feeling. At last she looked up at Jed.

"I don't want to write some silly column about spending a dream weekend with a famous baseball player, Jed," she said. "That's not why I've been bugging you for the last month. I want the real story, the big one, the reason why you hide from reporters, why you're afraid to be with me now."

"There is no story," he said flatly. "Except in your imagination."

"I think there is," she said quietly. "So does Charlie Huff. We can't both be wrong."

"Sure you can. You are. Both of you. I'm a dull, boring guy, Con. I don't do drugs. I don't drive fast, sporty cars. I don't hang out till all hours with a bunch of baseball groupies. I get up in the morning, go to the ballpark, work out and pitch. That's it, Con. End of story."

She studied him with narrowed eyes. Was that all there was to Jed Duval? For some reason, she didn't think so. There was something in him, some distant part he never shared with others. That was the part she wanted to find out about, the side she wanted to examine.

"I'm sorry, Jed," she said softly, "but I don't buy your line. You're an enigma, and that drives me crazy. I want to find out everything about you I can. I want inside your skin, Duval. I won't be satisfied till I get there. I want to know all about Jed Duval, about his dreams and fears, his secret yearnings, his most cherished aspirations. I want to get inside you. I want to hear your heartbeat up close, to ride with your blood through your veins, to sit in your gut before you pitch a big game. I want it all, Duval, and I won't be satisfied till I get it.''

His gray eyes took on a smoky cast as he studied her. "You make that sound sexy, Con," he said at last, his voice low and husky. "Like making love in the dark."

She felt shivers feather over her skin, felt the pulse in her neck begin to pound. She was suddenly conscious of her breasts rubbing against the lacy material of her bra, felt her nipples harden, aching for a man's touch, but not just any man's—Duval's. His smoky eyes seemed to reel her in, dragging her closer and closer to some dangerous place where everything was dark, where words were whispered and sighs echoed in cool night breezes.

She dragged her eyes away and struggled to keep her breathing even. "Don't make it more than it is, Duval," she said, her voice betraying her by sounding lush and quiet, like the muffled sound of violins on a foggy night.

"Don't make it any less," he murmured.

His voice seemed to caress her, stroked her shoulders, kissed the soft skin of the side of her neck, whispered over her lips, touched her eyes, her throat, the throbbing tips of her breasts. She took a breath and was embarrassed to hear that it was shaky, tremulous, like a young girl on her first date.

"Now who's the nervous one, Con?" Jed asked softly, his eyes filled with heat.

"I thought you didn't like me, Jed," she said.

"That doesn't stop me from wanting you."

"You want to make love to a woman you can't trust and don't like?"

"It's crazy, I know," he said, shrugging muscular shoulders. Her eyes were drawn to them. She shivered at the thought of touching Duval, of sliding beneath cool sheets to lie against his body, feeling his smooth skin under her hands.

Suddenly she wanted that. The desire to write a story receded, became something unimportant, trivial even, when compared to this new need. "What would happen afterward?" she asked softly.

He smiled. "Women always worry about that. Why worry, Con? Just let things take care of themselves."

"Sometimes they don't. Sometimes there are problems—like when it came time for me to write a story about you, Jed."

"You mean you'd let a thing like sleeping with me bother you?" he asked, his mouth curling into an amused smile. "You surprise me, Con. I thought a hotshot reporter like you'd just roll over and start typing before the sheets even had a chance to cool down."

She let his contempt roll off her, tilting her head at a curious angle. "Why do you dislike reporters so much, Duval? Did someone write something about you once that hurt you somehow?"

He chuckled humorously. "Con, no reporter even looked at me till I got to Boston. In the minors I was just a big, dumb country boy, throwing a smoking fastball and shoveling food in his mouth."

"Is that how you think of yourself?" she asked quietly, staring at him as if seeing him for the first time.

"That's how reporters think of me," he said, an edge of bitterness in his voice.

"I don't," she said. "I look at you and see an attractive, intelligent man. You're very quiet, of course, and that makes it difficult to know what you're really thinking and feeling."

"Why does it even matter?" he barked. "Dammit, I'm just a man, Con, not some silver-plated hero. I don't have wings and I don't fly. Why can't you leave me alone and let me be?"

"Because like it or not, you are a hero, Jed. I'm sorry, but you did it to yourself. If you didn't want to be a hero, you should have lost a few games last year."

He half smiled. "It crossed my mind."

"But you didn't do anything about it," she said softly.

He stared at the tabletop. "No," he said, looking up and meeting her eyes. "When you play baseball, you play to win."

"Even if it makes you an idol," she said softly, "and ruins your life."

He gazed unseeingly into the distance, and she wondered if he was back on the mound, hearing the roar of the crowds, feeling the eyes of a nation on his back, smelling the good smells of sweat and resin and newly mown grass at Barons Field.

"Sometimes I think there's a price every man has to pay for being alive," he said at last. "Sometimes I think we're all here on earth as some sort of punishment."

She felt a lump grow in her throat. He looked so lonely, so utterly isolated, burdened with fame he hadn't wanted, unable to cope with the demands placed on him by fans and the media. For the first time, she was in his skin and feeling his pain. She felt unexpected tears rise up behind her eyes and she had to blink them away. There was nothing to say, and even if there were, she had no right to say it.

Mutely, she reached out and put her hand on his. To her surprise, he turned his hand over, palm up, and closed his fingers around her hand and held it, clasped it as if it were all he had to hold onto in the world. In that moment, she began to fall in love with him.

STARTLED BY HER NEW awareness of Jed as a man, Connie couldn't come up with scintillating dinner conversation. Jed was a man of few words anyway. Consequently, dinner was awkward. They didn't say much, but were excruciatingly aware of each other. She reached for the salt only to encounter Jed's hand.

"Oh!" she said, drawing back her hand as if she'd touched a hot iron.

"You wanted the salt?" he asked, his eyes meeting hers then skittering away. "Here."

She took it from him and felt her fingers brush his. A tiny ripple of awareness fluttered through her, like wind blowing across a pond. "Thank you." She hated how she sounded—stiff, formal, like a Boston Brahmin at high tea.

"That's okay," he said. She had to hide a smile. He sounded like a kid. His hands were large, dark-skinned, beautifully formed, with short, blunt nails that were scrupulously clean. She thought of those hands caressing her naked skin, imagined them moving over her stomach, cupping her breasts, and felt a strange yearning deep in her midsection. She wanted those hands on her body tonight, wanted him to turn out the lights and creep into her bed, turn her to face him, slide his hands under her silken nightgown, seek her hot skin with his lips and tongue.

"Would you like dessert?" he asked, interrupting her torrid thoughts.

She blushed, fire red, to the roots of her hair. "N-no..." She forced a polite smile. "No, thank you."

He tapped his fingers on the tabletop. She thought she heard him whistle through his teeth. He looked on edge, ill at ease, as if he were worried about things over which he had no control.

"Would you?" she asked.

"Would I what?"

"Like dessert."

He didn't look at her. "If they had a slice of apple pie, I'd eat it."

She shivered. She wished she were a slice of apple pie.

She moved restlessly in her chair, trying to get her mind off the image that came to mind. "Ask the waitress what they have for dessert, why don't you?"

He sighed. "I'm not hungry for dessert."

She couldn't help it, the words came out before she could stop them, in a voice low and throaty, pulsing with sexuality: "What are you hungry for, Duval?"

He looked at her then, his gray eyes stabbing her and pinning her down. "Something I doubt you'd be willing to give a man."

"Why don't you try me?"

"I thought you said you'd never sleep with me to get a story."

"Who said anything about a story?"

He shook his head, his eyes cynical once more. "No way, Con. I'm not even going to think about it. That way lies trouble."

She told herself to stop flirting with him. She put her elbow on the table and rested her chin in her hand. "Where'd she go?" she asked, looking for the waitress.

"She's around," he said. "Why? You getting tired, or just bored?"

"I don't think I could ever get tired of being with you, Duval," she said, her lips curved into a slight smile. "I've been on your trail for a month now, and I haven't even discovered a millionth of what I want to know about you."

"Like what?"

She didn't know why she said it, but she did. "Like what are you like in bed?" Her voice was soft, low, throbbing with sensuality. "How do you make love to a woman?"

"I thought you wrote for the *Courier,* Con, not *Playgirl.*"

"Those were personal questions, Duval, not professional. I stopped being a reporter about half an hour ago."

"What happened?"

"I began to be aware of you as a man. I guess I figured if I'm not going to get the story I want, I may as well enjoy myself as a woman."

His gray eyes seemed to fill with smoke. "What do you like?" he asked, his voice low and intimate.

She shivered. "There hasn't been a man in so long, I couldn't tell you."

"Try to."

She picked up her wineglass and sipped the wine, staring at him over the rim of the glass. "I'm sorry," she said, setting the glass down. "I got out of line. I shouldn't have said any of that."

"But you did say it," he said. "Why?"

She shrugged. "Who knows?"

A smile hovered on his lips. "You're a tease, Connie Kenyon. You come on strong, then get scared and back off."

"You're right," she said, nodding. "Exactly right. I do get scared, Duval. And I am backing off."

"I don't think it's a story you want, Con. I think it's me."

She felt herself grow dizzy from the force of his words. Was he right? Is that what motivated Connie Kenyon? Mere lust? She forced a sardonic laugh. "Lord, you've got a big ego, Duval."

He shook his head. "No, I really think there's more to this than you're letting on. It might have started as an assignment, Con, but it's more than that now. You just won't admit it."

"You only wish." She wouldn't look at him. She sipped her drink and pretended he didn't exist.

"No, you do. You've been sitting here for the last half hour like you were scared to say anything for fear we'd end up in bed together. Relax, Con. They're only single beds. I need a bigger playing field."

She let out a shaky breath she hadn't realized she was holding in. "What do you have out on the island? A queen-sized bed?"

He shook his head, his eyes smoky. "King."

She felt the shivers roll over her like fog rolling over marshy land. She sat back and rubbed her arms. "Look, I'm going to take a walk. I'll be up later."

"I won't attack you tonight, Con," he said softly. "You won't have to sleep in your street clothes. You don't need a gun or a knife to protect yourself. The only thing you'll have to worry about is if you decide to crawl into bed beside me. Because if you do, I'll make love to you, like you've never been made love to in your life."

She shivered, but she couldn't look away from his eyes. They were dark and smoky, like fog in a storm. She lifted her chin and rose from her chair. "Don't stay awake waiting, Duval," she said coolly, then turned and walked out of the dining room.

Outside, she began shivering and couldn't stop. She stood against the trunk of a maple tree and wrapped her arms around herself, listening to the ocean crash against the rocks across the street, relentlessly booming, like the primordial echo of dinosaurs racing across the earth.

She wondered what it would be like to let herself go
and just be a woman with Duval, as natural and wild
as that ocean crashing onto the rocks. She wondered
what it would be like to give in to the passion pump-
ing in her veins.

She wondered what it was about Jed Duval that
made her face the truth: ambition wasn't enough. She
needed more in life, some*one*.

She wished she could walk into the inn and go up
those dark stairs and climb into bed with Jed Duval.
She wished she could lose herself in his arms, stop her
brain from working, her thoughts from forming in her
head. But she knew she couldn't; she needed more
than sex. She longed for love, intimacy, sharing,
communication. She'd always thought they were impossible to have, if she pursued a career. No man
could share her and her work; they'd want her to quit,
give it all up, become a shadow of her former self. But
maybe that wasn't so; maybe some men wouldn't be
threatened by her outsized ambitions. Maybe somewhere, there was a man she could share her life with.

Turning, she looked back at the inn. She saw the
window in their room. It was dark. She stood staring
up at it, wondering where Duval was—in the shadows
on the porch, watching her? Drinking in the lounge?
Watching television alone in the inn's den? Reading a
book in the library?

As she watched, she saw the light go on. Her heart seemed to stop, then raced on. She stared up at the window for a long time, then saw the light go out. He had either left the room or was in bed. She waited for another half hour, then went upstairs.

Chapter Eight

She opened the door as quietly as she could, easing it open, and jumped when it squealed protestingly on its ancient hinges. She held her breath, peering into the darkness, then heard Jed's even breathing. She closed the door quietly and turned the key in the lock, smiling sardonically to herself: the thing she had to fear was in here, not out there.

She groped in the darkness for her small suitcase, opened it soundlessly, rummaged around until she found a lightweight white cotton gown and her cosmetic bag, then tiptoed to the bathroom and got ready for bed.

She dusted herself with lilac-scented talcum and brushed her hair a hundred times, slowly, as if entranced by the rhythm of the brush, then stepped into a frilly white gown. It was a long lightweight cotton, so sheer it was almost transparent. Pale pink ribbons lined the low-cut empire neckline. She stood staring at herself in the mirror, wishing she'd brought something less revealing, but she hadn't expected to share a room with Jed, only a remote cabin.

Taking a steadying breath, she eased open the bathroom door. The bathroom light lay across Jed's bed like a ribbon from a flashlight beam. Her bed lay on the other side. She'd have to go around him, tiptoeing lest she wake him up.

"Well?" a voice growled roughly. "What the hell are you waiting for? Daylight?"

She jumped, her hand going to her racing heart, then she quickly turned off the light. "I didn't want to wake you," she said lamely.

"Well, you did," he barked.

She lifted her chin and marched around the end of his bed and lifted the sheets of hers. "Sorry," she snapped.

"You don't sound it."

She slid beneath the covers and pulled the sheets up to her chin. "I'll take up acting lessons tomorrow," she retorted.

"Don't bother," he snarled, turning on his side away from her. He made a great show of rearranging the covers, then sat up and turned on the light, swearing under his breath. "I was sleeping like a top, and you had to wake me up."

She glared at him coldly. "I'm sorry. Tomorrow we won't have this to worry about. Now turn off the light. I'm tired."

"Well, I'm wide-awake!"

"Then kindly leave," she said icily, and turned on her side away from him.

"I'm paying for this room, Hotshot. If anyone leaves, you do."

She turned over, her eyes blazing. "I'll pay half, if it's so upsetting to you. Good grief, Duval, I said I was sorry I woke you up. What more do you want? A signed apology?"

He raked his hand through his hair. "Okay, I'm out of line. I'm sorry, too." He looked at her with serious eyes. "You're so damned beautiful, Con," he said softly.

She stared at him, feeling shivers travel over her skin. "I'm a reporter, Jed. I'm here to do a story on you."

"Forget your job, Con," he coaxed in a soft, sexy voice. "Stop fighting it."

She took an unsteady breath, feeling her heart hammering beneath the soft cotton of her gown, aware of the yearning inside her, the sweet call of attraction and desire mingling with the smell of his after-shave. But something else called to her also, something just as sweet, just as necessary to her. She couldn't turn her back on all she'd invested, couldn't stop being who she was, no matter how tempting the man was who coaxed her to forget her own needs.

"Forget your job," Jed had said.

All her life she'd heard those words in some form or other: "Forget trying to be somebody," her father had sneered. "Who do you think you are? A princess?" "Forget trying to have a career, Con," her mother had warned. "You'll get married and won't have time for work any more than I do."

She heard the voices as clearly as if they were in the room with her and Jed. And here was Jed, joining in the perpetual chorus: Forget your job. . . .

She lifted confused eyes to Jed. "I can't."

He said nothing, just stared at her, then nodded. "Okay, I was out of line again. I'm sorry."

"All we seem to do is apologize to each other."

He turned off the light and lay down, his back toward her. "Good night, Con."

She gazed at his back with sad eyes. "Good night, Duval."

She lay back and stared at the window near her bed. The sound of the surf crashed ashore across the street, the breeze whispered in the trees outside, crickets chirruped in the garden, the window shade blew in on the breeze, then flapped back against the windowsill, the curtains fluttered. It was a long time before she slept.

SHE WOKE UP TO FIND him lying in his bed, watching her. She blinked, then pulled the sheet up, embarrassed that her nightgown had slipped down, revealing the soft swell of her breasts. "Enjoying the view?" she asked coolly.

He smiled and stretched, yawning amiably. "You bet."

"Are all baseball players so immature," she asked icily, "or do the Boston Barons just have a monopoly on men who are really boys."

"Aw, come on, Con," he said, grinning with a delicious lift of the right side of his mouth. "No boy I know would dream of thinking what I've been thinking, watching you."

"Oh, please," she said coldly. "Stop with the macho stuff, will you? It's boring, Duval. Boring and unconvincing."

"Now, don't tempt me, Con," he warned good-naturedly. "Don't make me show you what I'm talking about."

She flung back the covers and pulled a blanket around her. "Come off it, Duval. You're making me ill." She picked up her suitcase and headed for the bathroom. "I'm going to get dressed."

He grabbed her free hand as she sailed by his bed. "Hey," he said softly, "how about a morning kiss?"

She glared down at him. "I have bad breath."

He laughed out loud, releasing her hand. "Well, don't let me stop you then, honey. Get in there and brush those pearly whites."

In the bathroom doorway, she turned to look at him sourly. "I imagine you have it too, Duval, so don't be so cocky."

He grinned at her. "Million-dollar pitchers don't get bad breath."

"No," she snapped. "They just smell all over." She slammed the door, then bristled as he roared with laughter.

"Will you shut up?" she yelled through the door.

In answer, he just laughed harder. She glared at herself in the mirror, then whipped out the toothpaste and her brush and worked on her teeth till they gleamed.

"Breakfast?" he asked, when she emerged from the bathroom five minutes later.

"I'm not hungry," she said coolly.

"Well, I'm starving," he said. "But suit yourself. All meals were included in this dream weekend, though. I'd take advantage of it if I were you." He cocked his head as he looked at her consideringly. "You look like you could use a few good meals."

"Are you saying you don't like the way I look?"

"Honey, I love the way you look, but a few pounds in the right places wouldn't hurt you any. I can never understand what you women get out of being so skinny."

"I'm not skinny," she retorted. "I'm slim."

"Whatever," he said amiably. "I have to admit, though, you look real good to me."

"Then why try to get me fat?" she snapped.

"Who said anything about fat?" he asked innocently. "I was just suggesting breakfast, that's all. The ferry doesn't leave till ten, and it'll take a while to get to Jade Island. It makes a couple stops at other islands before it gets to mine."

"What's the matter? Don't you have any food out there?"

"Everything we need," he said. "Fish and biscuits and a few bottles of good wine."

"What about vegetables? If you're so concerned with my eating habits, I want fresh vegetables and fruits."

"Fine. We'll stop in the store and get some."

She looked him up and down derisively. "I can see this is going to be a great weekend."

"You are the most sarcastic woman I've ever met," he said.

"Maybe because you've hardly met any, Duval. You're too busy pitching."

"Looks like you've been digging into my past."

"Ha. What past? I'm convinced you sprang from a rock two years ago."

"So you have been bird-dogging me."

She lifted a shoulder. "Hey, I'm a reporter, trying to get a story. What can I say?"

"Okay, so if you're going to do a story on me, I guess we better get started, eh? What do you want to know? My favorite breakfast cereal?"

"Cheerios."

He stared at her incredulously. "How did you know that?"

"I checked your garbage."

He stared at her as if she were an insect on a dinner plate. "Let me get this straight, Con. You checked my *garbage?*"

She sighed. "Look, I have a job to do, okay? Don't get so high and mighty on me. You're not all that pure, either. You throw at batters intentionally."

"What other underhanded tricks have you got up your sleeve, Con? Concealed tape recorders? If we'd slept together last night, would you have recorded everything?"

"See why it was so important for us not to sleep with each other?" she asked, pointing at him. "Huh? Can you see why now, Duval? This has got to be strictly business between us. I've got a job and you're it. So stop hitting on me, okay?"

"Believe me, I won't come near you if I can help it," he snarled. He opened the door, then slammed it behind him. The sound echoed throughout the inn.

Good, Con thought darkly, with Duval around making so much noise, the other guests wouldn't need an alarm clock to wake up. The only trouble was, when was *she* going to wake up? For a while there last night, she'd actually indulged in fantasies about making love with him. That would have been about as smart as sleeping with a tarantula.

"HEY! DON'T I KNOW YOU?"

Jed looked up to find an overweight red-faced man beaming down at him over the breakfast table. He glanced at Con, then cleared his throat. "Well, I don't know you, sir," he said politely.

But the other man was nodding, his eyes narrowed assessingly. "Yes, I know who you are! You're Jed Duval!"

Jed sighed. "That's right."

"Look, could I have your autograph? It's for my little boy. He's crazy about you. Martha?" The man motioned to a plump woman seated at a nearby table. "Come on over, honey. Meet Jed Duval."

The rest of the diners turned to stare. A few said Jed's name out loud. Some laughed. Someone else got up and approached their table. "Say," he said. "Could I have your autograph?" He shoved a table napkin under Jed's nose. "Just sign this, Jed. To Gene. Make it out to Gene."

Jed scrawled something unintelligible on the napkin. The man frowned down at it. "Hey, you forgot the 'To Gene' part."

"Sorry," Jed said, pushing back his chair and rising. He bent down and scribbled on two more people's menus. "Sorry, I have to go." He met Con's eyes. "I'll meet you in the car."

She nodded and sighed. So this was what it was like to be famous? No wonder Jed didn't like it.

The overweight man who'd first spotted Jed was studying his autograph. "Can't really tell it's Jed Duval's," he said petulantly. "Hell, it could be Warren Spahn's, for all I can tell."

"It's Duval's," Con said, rising from the table. "You're a very lucky man."

The man brightened. "Hey, you're right!" Then he pursed his lips. "Wonder how much this thing is worth?"

Con dropped a tip on the table. "Now? Not much. Hold on to it, though. In thirty-forty years, it'll be worth a mint." She turned her back and left the dining room.

She found Jed at the desk, paying his bill in cash. "You included the breakfasts?" he asked, handing over two crisp hundred-dollar bills.

"Right here, sir," the desk clerk said, pointing to the bill.

Jed grunted, then turned to see Con. "Come on," he said, taking her by the arm, "let's get out of here."

"No wonder you don't like this part of it," she said when they had packed up the Blazer and were headed toward the general store. "Is it this way wherever you go?"

"When they recognize me it is," he said. "People aren't used to seeing me out of uniform."

"But Bozo back there recognized you."

Jed sighed. "Yep, he sure did." He glanced at her. "Now you see why I hate it?"

"But surely you must have realized this could happen when you got to the majors."

"Funny thing is, I didn't. I thought I'd be just another guy playing ball. My record in the minors wasn't all that great, Con. But something happened when I got to the majors." He frowned as he considered his words. "There are some men who can't perform in the limelight. The pressure gets to them. Me, I thrive on it. It's as if I needed to get to the big leagues to come into my own. But I hadn't realized that about myself."

"So all this is really a surprise to you," she said slowly.

"Surprise? Try shock. Hell, Con, no pitcher wins every game he pitches. Nobody *can*. Even on his best days, a pitcher depends on his teammates to hit for him, to get some runs, and usually that doesn't happen all the time. But whenever I pitch, I seem to have overpowering stuff and my teammates get hits. The runs just seem to jump on that scoreboard. But no one was more surprised by all this than me. Hell, I been in shock most of the past year."

"Maybe that's part of the reason why you haven't wanted to talk to reporters," she said slowly. "Maybe you're still not sure about any of this."

"Sure?" He laughed. "Honey, all during the winter I sat and stared into space. Oh, sure, I worked out to keep myself in shape, but I couldn't believe what had happened to me. Then I went back to spring training and I started doing it all over again. Winning. I guess it finally hit me toward the beginning of the season, back in early May, I guess, that this was for real. But am I used to it?'' He shook his head. ''No way. I just try to keep my head above water, that's all. Just try to keep from going under.''

She studied him as he drove. ''You're scared,'' she said softly, wonderingly. The thought had never occurred to her before.

To her surprise, he didn't react. He seemed to consider that. ''Yeah,'' he said finally. ''At least I was. All last year. I just covered it up real good, I guess. Now, I'm beginning to cope with it better. I always knew I was good, Con, but in the minors it was like I was fighting myself. I kept shooting myself in the foot. I'd throw great for a few innings, then give up ten runs. I'd get down on myself. But something happened when I reached the majors. I guess I just said, 'Hell, Jed, what have you got to lose? Go for it.''' He shrugged. ''So I did.''

''And look where it got you,'' she said quietly. ''Probably into the Hall of Fame.''

He shook his head, his eyes smiling. ''Naw, not yet anyway. Takes a long time and a lot of good years of winning twenty games or more to make it to the Hall of Fame.''

''Do you want that?''

''Sure, every ball player wants that. Most don't get it, but we all want it.''

She snuggled into the corner and brought her feet up
on the seat, resting her chin on her knees. She sat like
that and watched him, seeing him, maybe for the first
real time. She rested her eyes on him, seeing the crin-
kles at the corners of his eyes, the groove in his cheek
where he grinned, the dark shadow of beard just under his even darker skin, the line of his lips, curved and
almost sweet, as tempting as cherries on a tree.

"You like what you see?" he finally asked, drawl-
ing, his voice filled with quiet self-mockery.

She nodded, her eyes serious. "I do like what I see,
Duval."

He glanced at her. "I vowed I'd never talk to a reporter, yet I find myself talking to you, opening up.
It's like I can't stop myself. I don't know what happens. You ask me something and I respond."

"Maybe we knew each other in a past life."

He chuckled, shaking his head. "I believe we only
get one chance, Con, one go-round. That's why it's so
important to do it right the first time. This is the only
chance we get."

"That's a pretty unforgiving philosophy, Duval,"
she said softly.

"Yep, but that's the way I see things. Maybe that's
why the pressure makes me perform. I know this is all
I've got."

She found herself staring out the windshield, not
seeing the road up ahead. She was inside her head,
thinking her thoughts, alone, fighting with herself. "I

guess this is all any of us has got, Duval," she said at last. She sighed. "That's pretty depressing."

"Why's that?"

She shrugged. "I haven't done much with my life I'm very proud of."

"You're the society editor on the *Boston Courier,* Con. Surely you're proud of that."

"Not really," she said. She put her legs down and sat up straight. She turned her head and looked out at the ocean as they rode by it. The water was dark blue, topped with white foam that splintered into the air as the waves hit the rocks on shore. Gulls floated overhead, squawking raucously. The air smelled salty and clean, like a kitchen freshly scrubbed.

"How come?" Duval asked. "That's something to be proud of, Con."

She didn't answer right away. She wasn't used to opening up, to talking about herself. "It's not enough," she said at last. "It's never been enough. I thought it would be when I landed the job, but I was wrong. Society is the laughingstock of the paper. The other reporters sneer at it, look down at it."

"Sounds like you do, too," he said quietly.

She nodded, morose. "I guess so. Respect is important to me, and being taken seriously. There's something burning in me, Duval, something that won't let me rest. It's like a fire in me, a burning. It just takes me by the throat and chokes me sometimes."

"That's why you want to write about me," Jed said. "You recognized me. We're alike, Con. We're two of a kind."

She turned her head and looked at him, stared at him hard. Yes. He was right. They were just alike, both fighting to prove themselves while trying to keep something from their past a secret. She smiled as she realized how simple it was. Jed fascinated her because she was really trying to understand herself. She must have thought that if she could find out every detail about his life, she'd somehow understand hers.

"Well, isn't that a bully revelation," she said at last, her tone ironic. "How's that make you feel, Duval? It isn't falling in love with you I'm after, it's finding out about myself."

Jed pulled the truck to a stop in front of the general store. He cut the engine and opened the door. Then he leaned toward her, his eyes filled with quiet amusement. "Honey, you can twist your reasons all around, but you haven't got me fooled. It might not be love, Con, but it sure as hell is sex. When you come to terms with that, you'll stop standing in the bathroom doorway like you did last night *thinking* about it and you'll just get in bed with me and *do* it, which is what we both really want."

He nodded decisively, then got out of the truck and slammed the door after him. Stunned, Con was left sitting in the truck, staring after him as he took the porch steps two at a time.

Furious, she scrambled out of the truck and went after him, racing up the porch steps and tearing open the door to the general store.

"Duval," she called out, bristling with anger.

"I'm over here, Con," he said mildly from the produce aisle. "You want to give me a piece of your mind, come over here and do it. Don't force the locals to listen."

Red-faced, indignant, she stormed through the store, elbowing her way past two elderly spinsters and a young expectant mother. She found Jed inspecting eggplants.

"Duval," she said in a low voice that vibrated with anger, "you can't just make that kind of statement and then leave."

"I did, though, didn't I?" he asked, sounding unconcerned.

"Duval, I don't have a lot of people skills. I've gone on my own way most of my life and just concentrated on doing what I had to do. I haven't had many what they euphemistically call 'relationships.' But I do know one thing—we're never going to get anywhere, personally or professionally, if we don't stop talking *at* each other and start talking *to* each other."

"What's that supposed to mean?" he asked, examining a green pepper.

She took the pepper out of his hand and slammed it down on the counter. "Look at me when you talk to me, dammit."

Startled, he raised his eyes and glared at her.

"Good," she said, her voice lowering. "That's a start."

He nodded angrily. "Who made it?" he asked. "You think if I hadn't said what I'd said we'd have had this conversation? Con, you've been running from the truth ever since the day we met. You're hiding behind wanting a story on me, when what you're looking for is a lot more important. Only you won't admit it. You're stubborn."

"Just like you," she snapped. "Who's the one who's so determined not to talk to reporters?" She shook her head, her eyes blazing with anger. "It's not me, Duval. It's you. Well, you're with one now, sweetheart, and you better get used to it. I'm writing a story on you, whether you like it or not." She picked up the pepper and slammed it into his chest. "See how you like *them* vegetables, buster."

Turning, she stalked out of the store.

Jed threw the pepper into the pile of vegetables and raced after her. He caught up with her across the street, where the ocean thundered against the rocks and filled the air with salt-scented mist.

"Con." He reached out and took her arm and swung her around.

She looked up at him with defiant eyes ablaze with anger. "What's the matter, Duval? Don't like it when someone won't talk to you?"

"Con," he warned, "I'm a patient man, but you're sorely trying my patience."

She lifted her chin derisively. "Tough."

His gray eyes flared out and for a moment he was very still, then he smothered a curse and pulled her roughly into his arms and kissed her hard. She squirmed and squealed in protest.

"You lowlife," she growled when she finally managed to push him away. She wiped her mouth with her hand. "Don't you *ever* try that again. Do you hear me?" She was shaking she was so mad, on fire with anger, molten with rage.

Staring at her, Jed stepped back. All his anger seemed to drain away. His eyes softened and his voice became gentle. "I'm sorry," he said, reaching out to touch her cheek. Then he hesitated. His hand paused in midair, halfway to her cheek. He stared into her stormy eyes, then let his hand drop to his side. "I'm sorry, Con. I had no right to do that."

As quickly as it had come, her anger evaporated also. She looked away, her eyes filled with infinite sadness. "Just don't do it again," she said quietly. "I don't kiss anyone unless I want to."

"You're a tough lady," he said, unable to keep the admiration from his voice.

"Sometimes you have to be. It's a rough world, Duval."

He nodded. "I know."

Their eyes met. She looked away first. "Maybe we better get those vegetables, Duval."

"Yeah," he said, falling into step beside her. "Guess we better..."

"WE'LL NEED OLIVE OIL," Con said as she sailed toward the produce section. "Can you get it, Jed? I'll get the vegetables."

"I'd rather get the vegetables," Jed said.

She turned and fixed him with exasperated eyes. "Can't you ever do one thing I ask without fighting me?"

He stood, uncertain, then lifted his hands and let them fall in a helpless gesture. "Okay," he said. "I'll get the olive oil."

Con savored the victory. She chose some ripe tomatoes and picked up a local newspaper, and two minutes later she found Jed standing in front of a row of cooking oils, a bottle of corn oil in one hand and olive oil in the other. He had the most perplexed look on his face, as if he'd somehow wandered into a strange land where he didn't speak the language. She stopped a short distance away and watched him. As she watched, she found herself beginning to smile.

He was a typical man—at home on the playing field, but utterly baffled by domesticity. Standing back, observing him but unobserved herself, she saw the vulnerability on his face, the complete lack of understanding. She could almost hear the questions going through his mind: Weren't they all the same? They were cooking oils, weren't they?

She almost laughed at the way he seemed to be metaphorically scratching his head, perplexed by the rituals of female domesticity. And she felt her heart swell with something like affection.

Slowly, she walked toward him and took the olive oil from him. "Olive oil," she said gently, "is better for you."

He looked into her eyes and she saw an enormous store of something she couldn't quite pin down— frustration, resignation, confusion perhaps? What was it in his eyes? She stared up at him, feeling her heart opening to him.

"I guess you're not a domesticated man," she said, smiling softly.

He shook his head, embarrassed, like a little kid who'd stolen cookies and had been found out. "I guess not," he murmured ruefully.

"It's nothing to be ashamed of," she said softly. "It happens to the best of your sex." She trotted off down the aisle. "Come on, let's finish the shopping. You might learn something."

THEY DROVE TO THE docks, groceries piled high in two paper bags, their suitcases in the back seat. The ferry was waiting, but a hastily hand-scribbled note had been added to the notice that had been thumbtacked to a post yesterday.

"Ferry will run at eleven this morning, not ten," it read. "Sorry for the delay."

Jed glanced at his watch. "We better get these things on board," he said, sounding grim.

"Well, I don't know what the rush is," Con said. Honestly, this dream weekend was turning out to be a dud. Jed obviously resented her. It was a good thing she hadn't bid on Jed expecting to have a wonderful time.

"It's almost ten," he said. "The ferry will be leaving in five minutes."

"What are you talking about?"

"The ferry leaves at ten," he said, busy unloading their luggage from the back of the Blazer.

"Oh?" she asked, trying to make a joke about it. "How do you know that?"

He gestured to the sign. "Says so right there."

She stared at him hard. Was the guy obtuse or just blind? "Oh," she said sarcastically. "Is that what the sign says?"

He sighed and looked back at her, his arms loaded with luggage. "Just make yourself useful, Con. We'll be leaving in a couple minutes."

"No, we won't," she said, shaking her head wonderingly.

"Con," he said, raising his voice, "the ferry leaves at ten!"

"Jed," she yelled back, "the sign says there's a delay today and it won't leave until eleven!"

He stared at her, stunned, then before her eyes, he seemed to turn a sickly shade of green. He looked at the sign, stared at it blankly, as if he might like to change it into something else or make it disappear entirely.

"Wait a minute," she said slowly. "You didn't read the sign. You couldn't have read the sign, otherwise you'd know..."

He turned abruptly and began walking toward the ferry. Con stood and stared after him, feeling out of balance, as if someone had come along and snatched her chair out from under her. She had a sudden image of Jed holding the registration card...Jed with the menu...in the grocery store...

Suddenly it all made sense. Everything fit, like the scattered pieces of a jigsaw puzzle finally coming together.

Jed Duval couldn't read.

Chapter Nine

She found Jed on the ferry, standing at the rail, look-ing out toward the small islands that were scattered offshore. He didn't look at her when she approached, just continued staring into the distance.

"Looks like you found your story, Con," he said at last.

She didn't say anything. She didn't know what to say. She was still trying to assemble this new knowl-edge, to put it all together so Jed Duval made sense. It was strange how you could think you knew a per-son, and then your understanding changed com-pletely when you found out something new about them. Finding out Jed couldn't read was like watch-ing a pile of building blocks collapse and scatter all over the floor. Now she was faced with putting them all together again, rebuilding her image of Jed Duval, based, this time, on fact, not assumptions.

"It's true, then," she said quietly. "You can't read."

"For all intents and purposes," he said shortly.

"What does that mean?"

He shrugged. "I know how to read street signs. I can tell a Stop sign from a Yield."

Her forehead was wrinkled into lines of incomprehension. "How could you get this far without being found out, Jed?"

He laughed bitterly. "I didn't talk to reporters."

She let that go by. "You mustn't have talked to anyone." She tried to comprehend what his life must be like—a never-ending lonely game of pretense, of hiding the truth from everyone, lest someone tell the truth and let out his secret. "You must be exhausted," she said at last.

"Why?"

"Simply from the effort required to keep up the front, to not let people find out."

"You get used to it," he said.

She stared unseeingly into the distance. She never had. Not really. Her life might look fine from the surface, but underneath her smart exterior, her carefully selected suits, there was a constant simmering fear: *"I'm not what I seem—this isn't the real me. I can't let anyone get to know me, because if they do they'll find me out...."*

Jed Duval had been right—they were two of a kind, both hiding something in their past about which they were ashamed. Maybe it was shame that fueled their desire to succeed. Maybe it made them run faster and harder than anyone else. Or maybe it just made them feel inferior, so they thought they had to work harder.

Con stared out at the distant islands, small green lumps sitting in the ocean, like the backs of dinosaurs emerging from their watery surroundings.

"Well, what do you know?" Jed said cynically, "I've finally found a way to shut you up. You're shocked, aren't you, Con? I can already see your mind working—what kind of story will this make? Will I get a shot at the front page?"

She rounded on him, her face contorted with anger. "That's not true! I haven't even thought about the stupid story. I was thinking—" She stopped, unable to go on. What could she say? "I was thinking about my own life? About how I've covered up and hidden my secret, too?"

"What were you thinking, Con?" he asked, his low voice filled with derision. "About how much you pity me? About how sad it is that people like me exist in the world? About what a shame it is I couldn't have had a decent childhood? Well, we can't all be like you, Con. We can't all get the breaks you got."

She was shaking she was so angry. She didn't stop to think. She just reached out and slapped him across the face, hard.

And then she realized what she'd done. She saw his face, saw the surprise in it, the shock that she'd struck him, and she felt revulsion for herself fill her. It writhed inside her, like a slimy serpent. Self-contempt smashed over her, like raging water surging past a dam. She closed her eyes and stood very still, trembling.

"I'm sorry," she said, her voice wooden. "I shouldn't have done that."

"There are a lot of things you shouldn't have done, Con," he said, contempt ringing in his voice. "You shouldn't have tried to get a story on me. You shouldn't have bid on me at the auction. Most of all, you shouldn't have thought you could handle this story, because it's obvious, Con—you can't."

Turning, he walked away.

She almost followed him, then stopped herself. What good would it do? Right now if she tried to talk to him, they'd only fight. She turned back to the rail and stared out at the islands. Maybe Jed was right. Maybe she was in over her head, out of her league.

But she knew she wasn't. She knew she was the only reporter in the world who could write this story; it was hers. She might be able to read, but in every other way, she and Jed were soul mates, kindred under the skin. She knew shame, knew what it was like to want to hide her past, to need to escape her past and make herself over. So far she had succeeded, but she wondered what would happen when someday somebody found out her secret.

She felt a shaky laugh catch in her throat. Stinging tears pricked at the back of her eyes. She blinked rapidly and pushed them back. It was ironic, but Jed was doing to her exactly what she'd done to him—making false assumptions. But she guessed that's what people did when they didn't know the facts. She'd brought his reaction on herself, just as Jed had brought his fate on himself.

Well, she thought, now everything had changed. She almost laughed. How ironic, to search and search for the key to Jed Duval, and have it come to this: she didn't want to write this story. She didn't want to be the one to expose his secret. Not that it was so horrible. She supposed there were millions of people in the country who couldn't read. There was no shame in that—unless, of course, you were the one who couldn't read.

How was she going to get through the weekend with Jed? Make polite chitchat, share his meals and his cabin? To even contemplate it was to dread it.

She stood at the railing and realized they were moving. Turning, she saw that the ferry was beginning to pull out from the dock. No one else had boarded. A single man stood at the helm. Art, she supposed, the ferry's captain.

Well, she thought dismally, *you're in for it now, Con.*

JADE ISLAND WAS THE most remote of the small islands that lay offshore. It was beyond the other smaller islands, so that it wasn't visible until Art had circled the other islands and headed for the open ocean. There ahead it lay, a jewellike green island dense with vegetation. Pine and spruce and fir trees grew in thick abundance. Here and there, silver and paper birch grew like ethereal spectors, their white bark like pale slashes against the darker green foliage. And at the summit, a modern angular cedar house with a soaring roofline sprouted from a clearing, the only civilization amidst complete wilderness.

"It's magnificent," she said to Jed, when he appeared at her side. They were approaching the dock that led from a small spit of sandy shore, which descended from large gray rocks massed on the island's perimeter.

His eyes crinkled with pleasure as he feasted on the island. "Yes," he said, taking a deep breath. "It is."

"How long have you owned it?"

"I bought it last October," he said, "right after the World Series. I came up here and saw it and made an offer that afternoon."

"Then it wasn't you who built the house?"

"No, it was already here. The previous owner built it. It was a real labor of love. They had to bring all the materials out by boat, as well as the workers. You can imagine the expense."

"It must have cost a mint."

He flicked a hostile look at her. "Do you want to put that in your article, too, Ms. Kenyon? The exact amount I paid for this place?"

She felt as if he'd struck her. Two patches of red appeared in her cheeks, burning there like the imprint of his palms. She turned away without bothering to reply.

"Now it's my time to apologize," he said from behind her. "I'm sorry. I don't know why I said that."

"You're afraid," she said, turning to look at him. "I represent everything you fear the most." She looked into his eyes and spoke softly, quietly, "Jed, I told you once I'd never write a story about you that you didn't first approve completely. I meant that. If you don't want this to come out, I won't write about it. It's as simple as that."

He looked at her askance, as if he couldn't quite believe she'd said that. "You just got the Jed Duval story you've been frothing at the mouth over for more than a month, Con. What do you mean, you're not going to write it without my approval?"

"I meant," she said quietly, "just what I said. I'm not out to destroy you, Jed."

"What are you after, then?"

She shook her head, smiling. "I thought we'd already established that—I want to understand you, so I can understand myself."

"Oh? Are you hiding some deep, dark secret, too?"

She was spared from answering when the ferry bumped into the dock. "Jade Island," Art called out. "Looks good, Jed."

"It does," Jed answered, then looked back at her, lowering his voice. "You didn't answer."

She parried his query with a sardonic response. "I'm the reporter, Jed. I ask the questions."

"And it's my place to answer them, I suppose."

She nodded, forcing a brilliant smile. "Exactly. Now lead me to that place up there. It looks like something out of *Paradise Found*."

"What's that?"

She shook her head, irritated at herself for using a literary allusion Jed would never understand. "A seventeenth-century English writer named Milton wrote a book called *Paradise Lost*. I was just playing with words. If that was Paradise Lost, this is Paradise Found."

"You've read it?" Jed asked, "This *Paradise Lost?*"

"Just bits and pieces," she said. "In college English." She laughed self-consciously. "It was boring to me, then. I guess I never realized the gift I had—to be able to pick up any book and read it." She looked into Jed's eyes, her own eyes filled with sorrow. "I guess I needed to meet someone like you, who realizes how precious it is to read, something I take entirely for granted."

He searched her eyes, his own eyes at first mistrustful, then filled with doubts, hesitation, as if he couldn't bring himself to believe her. She wasn't laughing at him? Ridiculing him? She actually understood what he felt? It was as if the idea of being understood was antithetical to him, as if all his life he'd expected only scorn and therefore had received it.

He looked away, burying his confusion behind flat eyes. "We're here," he said. "We may as well face it— we've got a weekend to spend together. I suppose we have to make the best of it."

"Thanks," she said sarcastically, "you make it sound like electrocution."

A hint of a smile flickered on his lips. "Well, sparks do seem to fly between us."

"Maybe if we keep the length of the island between us, we'll get by without killing each other," she said shortly, then brushed past him and made her way down the gangplank that Art had lowered to the waiting dock.

"Have a nice time, ma'am," he said, nodding politely.

"Thanks. What time will you be back tomorrow?"

"Well," Art said, taking off his cap and scratching his head, "if the ferry don't break down, I'll be here 'bout five."

Con stared at him, her blood turning cold. "What do you mean, if the ferry doesn't break down?"

Art shrugged. "Well, it's old, ma'am, and like most women, pretty peculiar. Sometimes it just refuses to run. Engine part breaks or some such thing. But don't worry, ma'am, we'll get you off this island, if I have to come out in a rowboat."

"A rowboat," she repeated, suddenly feeling faint.

Art chuckled. "You're lookin' a little peaked. You okay, ma'am? Don't you worry none. You're not stranded here. Though you're lucky it's not winter. I 'member the time I dropped the first owner out here and couldn't get back for a week. He just about froze to death and almost died of hunger." Art chuckled again, his crooked teeth flashing behind thin lips. "Got plenty of food, do you, Jed?" he called out. "Wouldn't die of hunger, would you, if somethin' happened and I forgot you out here?"

"We've got enough to get by," Jed said, handing Con the two bags of groceries. "Here. You take these. I'll take the luggage. It's heavier."

"Such a gentleman," she said, and turned abruptly on her heel and made for the trail that led up the hillside.

"Have a nice weekend now," Art called out.

Jed waved and called goodbye, but Con didn't even bother to turn around. She felt about as comfortable marooned out here on this island as she would have on a maiden voyage to the moon.

The trail was about a foot wide, but the surrounding evergreens encroached from both sides, brushing against her as she labored up the rocky surface. Soon she was sweating. The grocery bags began to feel like fifty-pound weights. When she reached a clearing halfway up to the house, she staggered to a stop and almost dropped the bags.

"You okay?" Jed asked.

He wasn't even winded. Irrationally, she felt like snapping at him. "I'm fine," she said shortly.

"You look kinda tired out," he said, his voice gentle, his lips twitching in a half smile.

"And you find that amusing."

His smile widened. "Well, a little, I have to admit."

She gave him a look designed to chill his blood. "I'm not a professional athlete, Jed. I don't run wind sprints every day and lift weights."

"Maybe you should. Investigative reporters, now, they have to be in shape to handle whatever comes their way."

"Yeah, like Woodward and Bernstein, I suppose. I'll bet they hiked all over deserted islands when they were investigating Watergate."

"I guess that was sarcasm," Jed said.

"Lord, you are perceptive," she said, wiping sweat from her face and trying to catch her breath. "How much farther?"

"Not that far." He nodded upward. "The cabin's just up there a bit."

"Up there just a bit" proved to take ten more minutes of huffing and puffing. When she at last arrived in the clearing where Jed's cabin was located, she was thoroughly exhausted. Her arms were shaking from carrying the grocery bags.

"Cabin?" she said when she at last spied it close up. "Jed, it's a mansion!"

"I think you're exaggerating a bit," he said, leading the way toward the cedar house.

"Well, it's a heck of a lot more than a cabin," she said.

It was a full-grown house, with sprawling wings and cantilevered decks, two stories high, with a central cathedral-ceilinged section that soared three stories toward the cobalt blue Maine sky.

Inside, it was no less impressive. The entrance floor was Mexican quarry tile. This led to a living room where a three-story-high granite fireplace dominated the room on one side, and wall-to-wall windows overlooked a breathtaking view of the ever-surging ocean and rugged Maine coastline. White leather couches and chairs sat in a conversation grouping near the fireplace. A telescope faced the ocean. Underfoot, a plush oriental carpet in rust, brown and navy felt as deep and soft as a bedspread. Sliding-glass doors led to the deck, where redwood chaise lounges and chairs sat ready for sunbathing. Jed opened a storage closet and put out the white linen-covered cushions. He set up a blue-and-white striped umbrella over the redwood table, and declared the weekend officially begun.

"No more fighting," he said. "We're here to help the orphans. Let's just put away the swords and enjoy ourselves."

"A truce?" she said, relaxed for the first time in what felt like days.

"A truce." Slowly, he extended his hand. "Shake on it?"

She reached out and took his hand. "Shake on it."

Her hand felt small in his, like a child's lost in a man's. Feeling suddenly confused, she tugged it from his strong grip and turned away. "It's absolutely beautiful," she said, going to lean against the railing and stare out at the breathtaking view.

"I'm glad you like it."

"How do you leave?" she asked, turning to smile at him. "If I owned this place, you couldn't pry me off the island with a crowbar."

"I come as often as my schedule allows," he said. "And when the season's over, I spend all winter out here."

"Doesn't it ever get lonely?"

"Not really. The ferry still comes out every other day. I go in with Art and have a few beers at the local tavern once a week and buy groceries. It's peaceful out here. And actually I don't get to stay all that long. Spring training starts in March, so the few months I do get are a welcome relief from the constant traveling while I'm playing."

"That must get to be a drag, going from one city to another all season long."

"You get used to it, but it makes coming here even nicer." His face lit up as he spoke, making her catch her breath at how handsome he looked. "Can I get you something to eat and drink?"

"A cola would be good," she said. "If you have one."

"One cola coming up," he said. "Be right back. You just sit and enjoy yourself. You paid for this weekend, so I'm going to make sure you end up enjoying it."

She stretched out on a chaise lounge and put her head back. Slowly, the stress she'd been feeling drained away. The sound of the surf pounding on the rocks far below, the singing of the birds, the soft sigh of the wind in the trees all combined to relax her tense muscles. She felt as if she'd stepped into a dream world, where someone had been paid to cosset her and meet her every need. Even the muscles in her neck that had felt so tense were beginning to relax.

And when Jed came back, carrying a tray with a glass of cola and ice and a heaping tray filled with cheese and crackers and a bowl of shrimp sitting on ice, next to a small container of cocktail sauce.

"Mmm," she said, sitting up. "This must be what heaven's like."

"I guess the only thing that's missing are my wings," Jed said, smiling.

She narrowed her eyes and studied him. "If I squeeze my eyes almost shut," she teased, "I can almost see them on you. And a lovely halo shining around your head."

"That'd come as a surprise to all the reporters who like to call me Devil Duval."

"The other reporters don't know you as well as I do," she quipped, then regretted what she'd said. She glanced at Jed and saw that he was trying to ignore the underlying meaning.

"Let's forget everything that's happened and enjoy ourselves," she urged softly.

He looked up and met her eyes. "If I forget who you are, Connie Kenyon," he said in a low voice, "I might do something very foolish."

"Like what?" she asked, her voice soft. She felt chills go up and down her arms. His eyes were hypnotic. They seemed to make a hundred promises, weave a dozen spells.

He reached out and tucked a stray curl behind her ear. "I might not be able to keep away from you," he murmured. "I might find myself wanting to keep you captive here, all for myself."

She looked down, feeling a pink flush creep into her cheeks. Her heart was beating so hard she wondered if he could hear it. For some reason, the idea of being held captive by Jed Duval wasn't frightening in the least. It was tempting almost, even something to be desired. But she couldn't mix pleasure with business.

Looking up, she found herself smiling at him. "I doubt we'd last two days in the same house," she said, trying to defuse the sexual tension that suddenly seemed to shimmer around them.

"Well, we're going to get a chance to find out," he said, and stood up. "Let's make the most of it, Con."

She felt a strange thrill run through her. She told herself not to make more of the statement than Jed had meant. Still, she had a hunch this could turn out to be a weekend she'd remember the rest of her life.

Chapter Ten

They set out on foot to explore the island. Con was wearing jeans and a T-shirt, with hiking boots. Jed wore baggy khaki trousers, an old flannel shirt, the nap of which was completely worn away, and black tennis sneakers. He jammed a sweaty misshapen Barons baseball cap down over his head, picked up a fishing pole and tackle, and gestured for Con to follow him.

"Where we going?"

"Exploring and fishing."

"I'm not a fisherman, Jed."

"I am," he said, grinning. "You don't have anything to worry about. Just sit back and enjoy the ride."

Out here, a mile offshore, the air was clean and pungent with the odor of salt, rockweed and balsam. The sky overhead fairly crackled with brightness. It looked as if an ambitious housewife had scrubbed it clean, hanging the sun back up high in the sky like a shining ornament, a tribute to her housekeeping efficiency.

Con breathed in deeply, inhaling the smells with enthusiasm. She felt new, made over, as if when she'd landed on Jade Island, she'd shed her old self and found a new one.

"Complete peace," she murmured, as Jed fixed bait to the fishing hook and cast his line into the ocean.

"Ayuh," he agreed, teasing her by falling into the tones of a native Down-Easter.

"Why Maine?" she asked, eyeing him speculatively.

He didn't answer for a moment. Watching him, she realized she liked that about him. He took his time formulating a response, as if her questions really mattered; they deserved more than a quick answer off the top of his head.

"It's about as close to wilderness as you can get," he finally said, "and still be within a few hours of Boston. I considered Vermont and New Hampshire, but Maine's got the ocean, and there's something about the ocean that reaches me. I just look at it and feel peaceful. It soothes me."

Con nodded, her eyes scanning the distant flat horizon. "When I was a kid, I'd spend every summer on the beach in Ipswich. I never got tired of it, watching the ocean. It fascinated me. Still does. I know what you mean about the peace—it seems to reach out and grab you. I used to go to the beach whenever things got rough at home. Somehow I always found the guts to go back. The ocean gave me that. Things never seemed as bad after I'd looked at the ocean for an hour or two."

As she talked, Jed frowned. He glanced at her from under the bill of his cap. "What was it like at home?"

She considered his question as she studied the horizon. "Strange. I grew up always feeling different. I'd visit friends, and their parents were always so friendly, then I'd go home, never knowing what to expect. It was always quiet, except when my father would explode. He'd do that quite regularly, every few months. In between, we kind of tiptoed around, afraid to make any noise in case it set him off."

"He wasn't happy," Jed said, a statement, not a question.

Con laughed, but she wasn't amused. "You could say that."

"What about your mother?"

Con's eyes were sad, filled with memories she'd rather forget. "Mom left when I was twelve. She never said a word, just packed a bag and took off one day. We never saw her again."

"Never?"

Con stared out at the water, as if, by watching it, she'd find the courage to talk about her past. "I tracked her down once, before I went away to college. She was living in a cheap hotel near Nantasket Beach.

She'd been pretty, when I was a little kid. Blond hair, pretty blue eyes. When I found her in Nantasket, she was hard. Even her eyes looked mean. She wasn't my mother anymore. I turned around and left her there and never looked back.''

Jed's frown had deepened as he listened to Con's flat voice. Lines creased his forehead. Quietly, he reeled the fishing line in and cast it out again, listening, not saying anything, but concentrating on every word, every nuance in her emotionless voice. When she finished speaking, he looked at her as if he'd never really seen her before. The past did that—it filled in the blank spaces, created a context, made someone suddenly more understandable.

He'd bet she'd made a vow sometime soon after seeing her mother that last time—that she'd never become like her, that she'd never slide downhill the way her mother had. And she hadn't, he could see that, how different she was. Con was classy. She had style, presence, a kind of strength that came from having overcome adversity. But now he couldn't help wondering what it had cost her in the way of energy, determination, endurance.

She'd said to him earlier today, "You must be exhausted from keeping up the front."

And now he realized why; *she* was exhausted. She knew what it was to work hard for something, to grit her teeth and dig in her heels and make something of herself. She knew the day-to-day lapses in confidence, had experienced the doubts, had sat alone in the dark and wondered if she could really do what she'd set out to do.

He hadn't known why, but he'd recognized they were kin under the skin. Con and he were kindred spirits, counterparts. They had come from the same place, though probably half a continent had separated them as they'd lived out their distinct pasts.

"You're very quiet," Con said, interrupting his reverie.

"Thinking," he said.

She slid her hands into her jeans pockets. "And?"

He glanced at her. "I was right—we're a lot alike."

She smiled and nodded. "Soul mates."

He shrugged. "Something like that, I guess."

She bent down and picked up a stone and heaved it into the ocean, watching as it sailed in a high arc and then descended, splashing mutely into its watery destination. "I like being with you," she said. "It's comfortable."

He nodded. There wasn't any need to say anything. He didn't have to; she'd just said it all.

"A lot of guys on the team have been hitting on you," he said abruptly.

Her teeth flashed in a grin. "They sure have."

"You haven't done anything about it."

She grew very still. "What do you mean?"

"I mean, as far as I know, you haven't taken any of them up on their...er...suggestions...."

Amusement flickered far back in her blue eyes. "That's right."

He glanced at her. "Why not?"

She raised her eyebrows. "I guess I haven't been interested enough."

"How come?"

She tilted her head, her eyes gleaming. "I guess I've had my sights on bigger game."

"Meaning me?"

"I've been after a story on you, haven't I?" she asked innocently.

"That's all it is? Just the story you want?"

She bent and examined the rocks that littered the small strand of beach. "You got it."

He harrumphed silently to himself.

She looked up. "Why? You gonna hit on me now?"

He glanced at her, his eyes dark, unreadable. "You wouldn't be able to get away if I did, now, would you?"

"Is that a threat?" she asked softly.

He shook his head. "Nope."

"Good. I don't like men who make threats. Any man who has to can't be all that good at what he's thinking of doing with the woman."

The corner of Jed's mouth lifted in amusement. "I guess you're right."

"I know I am."

Now he did grin. "I like you, Con. You've got style."

She grinned back. "I know."

"Confidence, too."

"Yup."

"Where's it come from?"

She shrugged. "After a while, you been on your own a while, you know you can make it. That makes for confidence, I s'pose."

He nodded. "Yes."

He'd caught four bluefish. He picked them up by their tails in one hand and they set out for the house. "Bluefish on the grill," he said as they walked side by side. "With a salad and some of those nice little red potatoes you got, along with green beans and sliced tomatoes, it'll be the best meal you ever tasted."

"Second best," she said, laughing. "Best meal I ever had was Ipswich clams, steamers and a cold Molson ale one summer day late in July. A cold front had come down from Canada and the air was cool and dry. The sun was just beating down on the beach and my shoulders were hot and turning pink. I found this little place right on the water and ate like I'd never eaten in my life before." She laughed out loud in pure delight at the memory. "Lord, that was good food!"

Jed grinned. "This'll be just as good. Afterward, I'll build a fire in the fireplace. The stars out here look bigger than on the mainland. I like to lie on the living-room floor and look up through the skylights. Feels like I'm drowning in those stars."

She had a quick image of them lying on the floor, naked, making love. She saw herself on her back, Jed astride her, saw herself looking up into the dark night, drowning in the stars as he made love to her. What would it feel like, with him inside her, and her lost in the stars?

"You look like you're dreaming of something wonderful," Jed said in a low voice. "Want to share it with me?"

She laughed out loud, low and throaty, feeling as if she were filled with some kind of extraordinary energy, a kind of golden light. "Yeah, I'd like to share it with you."

"Well?" he said, sounding almost impatient.

She just grinned. "I don't know you well enough to tell you what I was thinking about."

"You would if you told me."

She laughed and pushed her hair back from her eyes. "It's wonderful out here. I want to come back every weekend."

"I'll give you a key if you like. When I'm out of town, the place is yours if you want it."

She turned her head and looked into his eyes. "I don't know if it'd be as wonderful when you weren't here."

He grinned. "Probably not."

She smiled in response, her teeth flashing white, her nose wrinkling with pleasure. She wanted to kiss him. She wanted to go up on her tiptoes and kiss the man, feel his lips on hers, his hands on her back, pressing her into that hard body of his.

"Do it," he said softly.

"Do what?"

"What you're thinking."

She hesitated only a moment, then went up on tiptoe and kissed him. Her lips touched his, lingered there, feeling the softness of his lips, then she pushed away.

Afterward, he nodded. "I thought that's what you were thinking. You've got expressive eyes."

"They sound more like bedroom eyes to me," she quipped.

He smiled slowly, his eyes glittering with amusement. "That, too."

She sighed with contentment. "Make this last, Duval. Make two days stretch into twenty."

"You mean you wouldn't get bored out here?" he asked laconically. "Big-time reporter like you? You wouldn't miss the deadlines and hectic pace, seeing your name under the society column?"

She tilted her head and considered him. "Why do you do that? Why do you put me down like that? What've I done to you?"

He shrugged. "Forget it. Forget I said it."

"I can't. It's like this wall between us. I start to feel close to you and you slide it between us—this . . . what is it? This *attitude*."

"I'm sorry." He shook his head, his eyes scouring the landscape. "I guess it's just..." He shrugged, looking helpless, as if he didn't know how to express his feelings in words. "It's how I feel better," he said, frowning as he tried to explain himself. "I mean, sometimes you scare me, Con. You're so damned smart, so beautiful. Sometimes I feel inferior." He looked at her, his face serious. "Maybe putting you down is how I feel better about myself."

Her eyes filled up with tenderness. "Maybe so," she said softly. "But why would you need to? You're good enough just the way you are, Jed."

He looked at her, hope rising in his eyes like the tide coming in onshore. But he shook his head. "Hell, Con, I'm just a big ole rawboned country boy who can't even read."

"So, learn to read."

He didn't respond, didn't even move. He stared into the distance, then finally looked at her. "Sure. You make it sound easy. Maybe it was for you. You learned when you were a kid."

"You ever go to a literacy training place? Literacy Volunteers? Anything like that?"

He shook his head.

"Why don't you?"

He laughed bitterly. "Sure. Big-time, big-league pitcher Jed Duval just walks into a Literacy Volunteers office and says, 'Hi, I'm Jed Duval and I can't read.'"

"Why not?"

He shook his head. "Now you get real, Con."

"I already am." She smiled. "How about if I taught you how to read?"

"Sure. Like you've got time."

"I have time."

He shook his head. "Well, I don't."

"You're just scared," she taunted softly. "Big-league pitcher Jed Duval's scared to death to try to learn to read."

He rounded on her, his eyes sparkling angrily. "Okay, so now you've paid me back for not taking you seriously. Fine. Let's call it quits, okay, Con? We're even now."

"*A,*" she said.

He stared at her, uncomprehending.

"*B,*" she said.

He didn't say a word.

"*C,*" she said.

His face closed up. His jaw tightened. He looked like he was going to turn and bolt.

"You'll have to learn the alphabet," she said. "Once you get that, you've got it knocked." She was scared to death he'd walk out on her. She held her breath, waiting, tense.

He didn't say a word.

"*A, B, C,*" she said softly. "They're the first three letters of the alphabet, the foundation of all words. *A* is for animal. *B* is for boy. *C* is for . . . for Constance.

Each of those words starts with that letter of the alphabet." She reached out and found a stick and traced the outline of the letter *A* in the dirt. "*A,* the first letter of the alphabet. This is where we begin."

He stared down at the letter, his face a study in terror. She watched as he fought with himself and his fear, watched his face mirror his emotions—fear battling with his desire to learn to read. Finally, he lifted tormented eyes to hers.

"Okay," he said. "I'll try."

She let out the breath she'd been holding and smiled. "Good," she said softly. "That's all you have to do."

Chapter Eleven

"Buzz Drummond told me a story about you," Con said, as they were preparing supper. "He said you painted a bull's-eye on the side of an old barn and used to go out every day and practice pitching, trying to hit the bull's-eye. Is that true?"

Jed grinned. "Yep. There's this old, abandoned barn outside a little town called Prairie's Edge in Kansas. Never did find out who owned it. I painted the target on it and that's how I learned to control my pitching. I used to throw hard, but I wasn't very accurate. Ball would just breeze by the hitters, 'cept it'd be a block away outside. I worked on my pitching every morning for three hours, whenever I was in town. 'Course in the minor leagues, that wasn't very much, since you travel by bus, usually, and it's god-awful uncomfortable. Still, I'd get in about four mornings a week worth of practice. Damn target worked, too." He smiled thoughtfully. "I suppose it's still there."

"You ever think of going back and buying that barn?" she asked, smiling.

He laughed. "Wouldn't that be a hoot? No, I can't say I ever did, but it's an idea." He glanced at her, his eyes smiling. "Last year, I was so into my pitching I didn't think about anything till the season ended."

"How's it feel to know you finally lost a game? Is the pressure off now?"

"I never really felt a lot of pressure. Mostly it was the papers and the television people making a big deal about it." He glanced at her uneasily. "I'm sorry, Con, but I just don't think much of most reporters. In my experience, they'll do anything to get a story, and they don't care who they hurt in the process."

"That might be true of some reporters, Jed, but not all of us. Some of us are decent human beings. We have families to support, we vote, pay our taxes. You make us sound like ogres."

"Some of you are," he said quietly. He continued cleaning the bluefish, his head down as he worked quickly and efficiently with a boning knife.

Con rinsed the lettuce for their salad and shook off the water, her face thoughtful. She glanced at Jed. "What happened to make you feel that way?"

"Nothing, Con. Just forget it."

She watched him with compassionate eyes. "You have a hard time trusting me, don't you?" she asked softly.

He stopped eviscerating the fish and looked up, staring out the window over the kitchen sink at the ocean in the distance. "I'm sorry, Con, but trust doesn't just spring up overnight."

"You're right," she acknowledged. "I'm sorry. I don't have a right to pry."

"You finished with that salad?" he asked, changing the subject.

"All set," she said brightly. "You ready with that fish?" She was hurt, but she knew he was right. She hadn't yet proven herself to him. Didn't she know enough about mistrust to realize that?

"Con."

She looked up to find him watching her, his eyes worried. "Look, I'm not trying to make a big deal about this, but I can't help how I feel. It's hard to trust you. If I open up to you, I may find my guts spilled all over the front page of the *Boston Courier* some day."

She nodded, her face troubled. "I know that's how you feel, but that's not what's going to happen. But I understand, Jed. Let's forget it, okay? It seems like whenever we talk about my work, we get in trouble. We were doing fine before this started."

"Yeah, we've gotten through a whole afternoon without killing each other," he said.

She smiled. "Yeah, but just watch yourself, Duval. Better hide that boning knife, or you might wake up with it sticking out of your ear."

"Just as long as it's my ear and not my back," he said. "I don't think there's anything worse than being stabbed in the back by someone who's told you you can trust them."

"Jed, I made a promise. The only way you're going to find out I'll keep it is by letting time go by. You'll see. You're not going to wake up and find the story of your life splashed across the front pages of my paper."

"How will you explain not having a story to your boss?"

"Vinnie?" She shrugged. "I'll just say I couldn't do it."

"Couldn't do what?"

"Couldn't get a story on you, couldn't make you open up."

"But you did, didn't you?" he asked softly. "That must be a pretty bitter pill to swallow, knowing you've got the story but I won't give you permission to write it."

"Who says you won't?" she asked. "Hell, Duval, I'm going to use all my female charm on you. Didn't Charlie Huff warn you about that? Didn't he tell you I'd sleep with you to get this story?"

"But now you don't have to. You've already got it."

"But not your permission to write it," she said.

"Stalemate."

She shrugged. "Only if I fail in my womanly wiles."

He smiled, one corner of his mouth lifting in a slow grin. "You're a tease, you know that?"

"It's called flirting, Jed, in case you haven't ever engaged in any before."

"You do a lot of it? Flirting?"

"Not much. I haven't found all that many men I'd waste my time on."

"But you would with me."

She smiled, letting her eyes travel up and down his body. "You're not an ordinary guy, Duval. You're kinda special."

He grinned. "Cut out the malarkey, Con. We got fish to fry here."

"Fry? No way, Jed. Frying's bad for you. We're going to grill it on the grill. You're in charge. I'll do the vegetables." She patted him on the rump as she passed him. "Come on now, Duval. Let's get cracking."

A HALF AN HOUR LATER, they were seated at the redwood table on the deck. The sun was low in the west, layering brilliant colors across the water, turning the rocks on the mainland to gilt. Jed poured white zinfandel into Con's glass, then lifted his in a toast.

"To us," he said. "And this weekend."

"To us," she repeated softly, meeting his eyes.

"Damn it," he said, looking into her eyes. "Why do you have to be a reporter?"

"Would it make any difference if I were a computer programmer, say, or a waitress?"

"All the difference in the world."

She smiled. "Sometimes I think we meet the exact people in this world we need to meet so we can come to terms with our issues."

"Issues?"

"You know, the things that hold us back, that keep us mired in the past. Take you, for instance. You've got this thing about reporters. Maybe you had to meet me, or someone else like me. Maybe it was in the cards, so to speak. Kismet."

"And what about you? Did you have to meet me?"

She considered that. "Maybe. Maybe I needed to find someone I could—" She stopped herself just in time. Slowly, she raised her eyes to his. She'd been about to say, "Someone I could fall in love with." She sat and stared at him, really looked at him, saw his eyes and mouth, his strong chest and powerful shoulders, but she also saw more than that; she saw the man beneath the bones. Appearances were important at first, she supposed, but what really mattered was a person's soul, his heart, his values. Was she falling in love with Jed Duval? Was that what this had been about all along? Had Jed been right, that she'd really just wanted him and not the story?

"Someone you could what, Con?" he asked softly.

She took a shaky breath. "I don't know. I don't know what I'm talking about."

"I think you do. I think you're a lot more like me than you want to admit. You're scared, too, Con, but you're scared of falling in love."

She put her elbow on the table and fiddled with her hair. She brushed a crumb off the table. She picked up her wineglass and took a sip. She swallowed, then cleared her throat.

"Well?" he said. "Am I hot or cold?"

She smiled. "Lukewarm."

He shook his head. "I think I'm on fire," he said in a low, sexy voice.

She shivered. He sounded so good. She could almost taste his kisses, could almost feel his body against hers. She lifted her eyes and looked at him. "Okay, medium warm."

"You won't admit it, will you? What happened to scare you off men so much? Did you fall in love once and get hurt real bad?"

"Yes, but that's not the only reason. I guess I watched my parent's relationship, Jed. They were miserable together. They wore each other out. But I remember when I was just a little girl, my mother used to tell me how she'd loved my father so much when they first met. She used to say she would have done anything for him. And I used to wonder, how could it happen? How could you love someone so much and have it die? How did it die? What happened to them?

What made them come apart and start hating each other?" She shrugged carelessly, as if it didn't still hurt. "I vowed I'd never let that happen to me."

"But you're not letting anything happen to you, Con. You've locked yourself up and thrown away the key."

"Then I guess you'll have to find it, won't you?" she quipped.

"Don't, Con. Don't treat this lightly. What's happening to us is important."

She took another shaky breath. "You mean, it's not just sex on a summer night?"

"Do you think that's what it is?"

She shook her head. "No."

"Neither do I."

"So what are we going to do about it, Duval?"

He smiled, and in his eyes she saw warmth and laughter and the promise of good things to come. He picked up his fork and took a huge bite of bluefish. "Enjoy dinner," he said. "Now come on, Con, eat up. I cooked this just for you."

Smiling, she picked up her fork. She took a bite and murmured appreciatively. She had to admit it, the man sure knew how to cook....

WHEN THE SUN SET, it grew chilly on the deck. They went inside and Jed lit a fire in the fireplace. Soon it was crackling heartily and they were seated on one of the leather sofas, sipping the rest of the zinfandel. Soft music played on the stereo system. Overhead, the stars were visible through the skylights, like brilliant needles in a black velvet pin cushion. Moonlight illuminated the forest outside, casting ghostly shadows across the clearing in front of the deck.

"So your parents had an unhappy marriage and you're afraid to risk it," Jed said as they stared into the fire.

"No," Con corrected him, "I decided I wanted to do things differently, that's all. My father was a frustrated musician. He played sax. When he was young, he dreamed of making it big. Later, he met my mother and she got pregnant. He had to marry her. He always blamed her and me for holding him back. That was his excuse—if he hadn't had to get married and support a family, he'd have made it as a musician. He became increasingly bitter."

"What about your mother? Was she content to be a wife and mother?"

"Not really. She thought she would be, but as her marriage deteriorated, she got bitter, too. She'd been raised with the pie-in-the-sky notion that all your problems ended when you found a husband. Instead, that's when all her problems started. Before she packed her bags and left, she drilled it into me never to sleep around, that I might get pregnant and end up like her."

Con laughed sardonically. "Consequently, in high school, I experimented with a boy, but found out sex wasn't half as great as everyone made it out to be. Instead, I focused on my grades. I figured an education was a way out of that life. I haven't looked back, Jed. I've just kept walking, trying to put as much distance between my past and me as I could."

"Has it worked?"

She stared at the flames eating up the firewood. "Funny thing about that. It's with me all the time. I constantly dream about my childhood. I'm always back in that house I grew up in, trapped and trying to get out. I wake up scared to death, my heart pounding. Sometimes I want to tear my mind out of my head, just shred it to bits to stop the memories and the dreams."

Jed reached over and took her hand in his. "Sounds scary."

She curled her fingers around his and closed her eyes. She didn't want him to see how much she needed someone to understand. He seemed to, and for some reason that was scary. She was afraid to believe that someone could accept her for who she was. "Lots of things are scary," she finally managed to say, but her voice broke and she turned her head away.

Gently, he reached out and put his finger under her chin, turning her face toward his. "Con," he whispered. "Look at me."

She forced a strained laugh. "Oh, come on, Jed. Let's not get serious, okay? I hate being serious."

"But this is serious."

She shook her head. "No, it's not."

"You are so scared," he murmured, his eyes traveling over her face, seeing the vulnerability in her features. Her eyes were wide and filled with fear. She moistened her lips and cleared her throat.

"Jed," she said, sounding suddenly tired, "I'm just not good at relationships, okay? You're right—I'm scared. I wish I weren't, but I am. Those are the breaks, I guess. Maybe everyone has something they fear in life. For me, it's dependence on somebody else. If I let myself care for you, Jed, if I began to need you, I'd feel as if my whole life would fall apart. Right now, it works. I have a good job and I'm good at it. I have money in the bank and no debts and a nice place to live. I function well. With a man in my life, I'm afraid everything would start falling apart. I can manage by myself, Jed, but I think I'd blow it if I ever fell in love with someone."

"But that's what you're longing for."

"Don't we always want what we most fear?"

He considered that, then nodded. "Yeah, I guess so. I want to read and I'm scared to try."

"See? Then you have to let me take this slowly. Jed, I don't sleep around. A relationship, if I ever get in one, is too important to me. My mother went one way. Me, I chose the exact opposite way—I don't sleep with anyone. At least I haven't lately. There was one guy in college . . ."

"What happened with him?"

"I fell, hard. Head over heels. Heart palpitations. Stars in my eyes. The whole nine yards. It lasted six months and was pure passion. We were in bed more than we were out of it. Then he found someone else and left me. I was devastated. I vowed I wouldn't let it happen again. I'm attracted to you, Jed. I have been ever since I met you, but I'm damned if I'm going to fall into bed with you the first night we're alone."

"The second night," he corrected her. "We were alone last night, too."

She ignored his interruption. This was too important to make jokes about. "You can't trust me, Jed. Well, I guess I understand that, because I'm afraid to trust you, too. We're two people who've been hurt one too many times. We're afraid to trust, afraid we'll be hurt again. Well, let's just leave it at that, okay? Let's give ourselves time and see if we can learn to trust each other."

He rested his head against the back of the couch, staring into the fire. "Why's it have to be so damned hard for us and so easy for other people? That's what I want to know. Some of the guys on the team, they meet a pretty girl, date her, and before you know it they're married and have kids. And they're happy! They share their lives with someone, buy homes, take out life-insurance policies, start college funds for the kids. It's all so *nice*. Yet here you and I sit, attracted to each other and unable to do anything about it. It's sick, Con. Maybe we should just say the hell with it and take a chance.''

She shook her head. ''I don't want to jump into anything with you without having both eyes open. And I sure don't want to leave myself open to your charges that I slept with you to wangle permission from you to write the story.''

''Yet you teased me earlier that that's what you'd do.''

She nodded, smiling sardonically. ''Because I'm afraid that's what you'd think if we did sleep together and then you relented.''

Jed stared moodily into the fireplace. ''What do you think would happen if you wrote the story and people found out?''

She didn't answer right away. ''I don't know for certain,'' she said slowly, ''but I imagine most people would be very supportive. By and large, Jed, people are understanding when they hear about the tough times others have had in life. Sure, you get a few loudmouths who have an old shoe in place of a heart, but I truly think you'd find a lot of people rooting for you. Plus that, I think a lot more would come out of the woodwork and confess that they can't read either. I guess what I think could happen, at least in an ideal world, is that you might come to be a spokesperson for others who can't read. If you do learn to read, Jed, that could be more inspiring to people who feel hopeless than all the major-league wins you could tally in a ten-year career.''

"If I can learn," he said. "That's the question, Con. What if I can't?"

"Everyone can learn to read, Jed. If it's a question of a learning disability, like dyslexia, then you'd need some special assistance, but that shouldn't stop you. You're an intelligent, determined man, Jed. Turn some of that determination that got you into the major leagues to learning to read. You'll do it, Jed. I know you will. Then you won't have that shameful secret burning a hole in your soul every day." She smiled wryly. "Maybe you'd even begin to talk to reporters once in a while."

"What's that thing you mentioned? Dis—? What?"

"Dyslexia. I don't know all that much about it, but it's a disability lots of people have, where they don't see words the way others do. The letters get all mixed up, so they can't decipher the words. Then some people have what's called a learning-attention deficit. They're kind of hyperactive and can't concentrate like others can. But all of those things can be corrected, or at least worked with."

"I don't know," Jed said, shaking his head. "I think I just never stayed in a school long enough to learn. In first grade, I was in five different schools. I'd no sooner start to read Dick and Jane than Dad would pick up and move us again. I'd get to the next school and they'd be past that and I never seemed to be able to catch up. Instead of speaking up about it, I was scared and I just tried to pretend everything was okay. I got to be a master of deception. The teacher would call on me to read and I'd make a joke, or I'd pretend I was daydreaming and she'd yell at me and forget she wanted me to read. There were dozens of ways to get out of reading."

"Yes, but what about tests? How'd you ever manage them? And writing?"

He shrugged. "I'd skip school the day of exams. It never seemed to matter, because my Dad would pack up and move us again the next week anyway. He taught me how to write my name. If you can write your name, you can get by in the world. He taught me to identify street signs. I can recognize lots of words on signs. You get to recognize restaurants, gas stations, that kind of thing. I know the difference between McDonald's and Burger King. I listen to the radio a lot, and watch television. That gives me lots of information. You'd be surprised what you can get away with if you have to."

"But at how high a cost?" she asked softly.

He let out a sigh. "Yeah. It does get tiring, always having to watch yourself." He rubbed his eyes. "You know what feels good right now?" She shook her head. "Just being able to talk about it with you. It's like, *finally,* there's someone I can talk to. I don't have to keep the secret anymore, at least not with you. It feels like being let out of a cage for the weekend."

"I don't know, Duval, it sounds like you're beginning to trust me," she said softly.

"Maybe." He smiled. "I guess I won't know for sure until I see what kind of story you write next week."

"Let's see, I'll probably do an in-depth article on how certain Boston socialites spend their summer vacations. Something with a lot of meat in it, Pulitzer Prize stuff."

"No stories about dumb ball players, hmm?"

She met his eyes. "I don't know any dumb ball players," she said softly.

Leaning over, he kissed her. It was a gentle kiss, so sweet she felt like melting. "Good night, Con," he said, rising. "I'll see you bright and early in the morning. You know where your room is, the bathroom? Do you need anything?"

"I don't need anything," she answered, but as she watched him climb the stairs to the master bedroom, she felt like calling him back, telling him she did need something. She needed him.

Instead, she turned and looked into the fireplace, let herself be drawn into the power of the flames. She sat like that for hours, until the wood was just a pile of glowing embers in the grate.

Chapter Twelve

The next morning, dense fog swept in from the ocean, enclosing the island in white mist. No sun penetrated the heavy curtain, though sounds seemed magnified—the clanging of a bell on a buoy, the sound of the ocean splashing gently against the rocky shore, the dripping of water off the eaves.

"It doesn't look good," Jed said, peering out the kitchen window as coffee perked and eggs sputtered in the frying pan. "When the fog comes in like this, it sometimes stays socked in for days."

"Days?" Con looked up from flipping the eggs. "You mean we could be marooned out here for days?"

Jed shrugged, turning on the ham radio and listening to the spluttering static. An occasional unintelligible burst of garbled speech shattered the quiet, then the static returned. He turned it off. "I'll try to reach

Art after we eat. Maybe the fog will lift and he'll be able to come out and get us on schedule."

"And if he can't?"

"We stay."

"Oh."

Jed grinned. "You look worried. What's the matter, Con? Don't like the idea of being with me any longer than necessary?"

"Actually, I'd like having to stay out here awhile longer, if you must know. I like it here. You know that, Jed."

"How'd you sleep last night?"

"Like a top. There's something about walking all over an island that does the trick better than sleeping pills."

"I slept lousy."

"Oh? That's too bad." She looked back at the eggs and hurriedly turned off the burner and removed the pan. Suddenly, her hands were shaking and she felt nervous.

"Yeah. I kept thinking about you, remembering what it felt like to kiss you good-night."

She rubbed her palms on her jeans and looked around, trying to think what needed to be done next. She wasn't used to cooking for anyone. When she entertained, she kept her guests in the living room so she could be undistracted in the kitchen. She wasn't exactly Dorothea Domestic; never had been.

"You ignoring me?" Jed asked.

She looked up quickly. "No, I'm just scatter-brained in the kitchen. The eggs are done and the coffee's ready. Why don't we eat?"

"You are ignoring me," he said, smiling. "You look flustered, like you don't know what to think about what I said."

"I think you're a typical horny male," she said wryly. "Now sit down before the eggs taste like ice cubes."

"A typical horny male would have beaten your door down."

"Mmm," she said. "You've got a point there."

"I considered it."

"Why didn't you do it?"

"It isn't about sex, Con."

She looked up and met his eyes. "What's it about, Jed?"

"I don't know."

She smiled. "Exactly my feelings. I don't know, either. To tell you the truth, I didn't go to bed till way after midnight. I stayed downstairs and stared at the fire till it burned out."

"I know," he said. "I was awake till I heard you come upstairs, and long after, I'm afraid."

"Why didn't you come down and join me?"

"Because I wouldn't have been able to stop kissing you," he said. "I wanted to kiss you so much, Con, I was aching inside I wanted you so much."

"I thought you said it wasn't about sex."

"It isn't. Sex just happens to be part of it."

She stared down at the eggs on her plate. "Maybe we're fighting a losing battle," she said slowly. "Maybe we shouldn't try to stop it, if it's what we both want."

"That's what I've been thinking."

She lifted her head and looked into his eyes and felt her stomach dip inside her. His eyes were warm and his lips looked so good. She remembered how he'd tasted last night when he'd kissed her good-night. Abruptly she pushed her plate away and got up. She went to stand in front of the sink. She stood staring out at the white mist that enveloped the island.

"Jed," she said quietly, her voice trembling, "I won't write that story about you, I promise. You have to believe me. I've never wanted to hurt you or use you to make a name for myself. I think it's always been something a lot more personal." She turned around and met his eyes. "Jed, I'm tired of trying to control myself when I'm with you. I've wanted to kiss you so bad—"

He was out of his chair and across the room in an instant, sweeping her into his arms, kissing her desperately. She kissed him back, as desperate as he, shaking with need, feeling faint from the desire that swept through her. His hands were all over her, in her hair, up and down her back, on her hips, pressing her into his body, holding her as he tilted her head back and devoured her lips, his tongue tangling with hers.

She felt as if some dam inside her had burst, releasing all the pent-up longings. They swept through her joyfully. It was ecstasy to be held by him, kiss him, feel his body against hers. She was all sensation, pleasure cascading through her, urging her on. She needed more than kisses, longed for the ultimate fulfillment. He pressed his groin into hers and a wild, sweet ache pierced her, like pleasant pain. She throbbed for his touch, gasped when his hand slid between her legs and found her.

Clothes were a nuisance, an impediment. She broke their wild kiss and looked into his eyes. "Jed," she whispered. "Let's go upstairs."

He took her hand and led her up the stairs, down the open hallway that overlooked the living room below, and into his room. They undressed quickly, their hands shaking, fumbling with buttons and clasps. Naked, they stood looking at each other, then went into each other's arms.

The feel of his hard body was sweet torment. She closed her eyes and groaned softly. He picked her up and carried her to the bed, ran his hand lovingly over her body. He knelt over her and dropped his head to her breasts, opened his mouth over a swollen nipple, sucked it into his mouth, rolled his tongue over it.

She trembled, running her hands down his back, her eyes closed in ecstasy. Finally. At last. He was touching her, his naked body atop hers, his hands first gentle, then urgent, his lips everywhere, his tongue like a questing fire on her breasts, her stomach, her burning, aching womanhood.

She arched her back and gave herself up to the liquid joy that filled her. She wanted only one thing, to be joined with him, to have him inside her, buried in her, one with her, not separate. She felt the desire like an insatiable need, her body demanded it, called out, unsatisfied without him. Strange how desire could take over her mind, her body, her very soul, could make her hunger and thirst for him, crave him like food and drink.

And then he was inside her and she felt such joy, such wonderful happiness, as if her body, her very self were shouting: Yes! This is what I've wanted, longed for, this is what I've waited for all my life!

"Con?"

Afterward, Jed's gentle voice called her back from ecstasy. She opened her eyes and looked up at him. She didn't say a word, just looked into his eyes, feeling open, exposed. If he looked, he could see all the way into her soul. She knew it. There were no barriers, no walls, no separate identities. Having merged physically, for this brief instant she still felt one with him, floating in the aftershock of ecstasy.

She didn't know what to say. What did you say after something like this? What could you say? Could any words express the feelings that swelled inside her? She felt tears well up in her eyes. He reached out with a gentle fingertip and swept them away from her cheeks.

"Are you okay?" he murmured.

"Yes..." Her lips trembled. She put her arms around him and hugged him fiercely. "Oh, yes."

He hugged her, pulling her close, pressing her face into the curve between his shoulder and neck. "My God," he said.

She nodded, mute. She couldn't speak. Her voice wouldn't work. Her heart was too full.

He released her and went up on his elbows, looking down into her radiant face. "I hope the fog stays all week."

She smiled, then laughed, hugging him, closing her eyes, pressing the tears back. "All month," she whispered.

"All year."

She opened her eyes and looked up at him. "I..." She shook her head. She reached up and touched his cheek, traced the lush curve of his lower lip. "I want to touch every part of you," she whispered. "And I want you to touch every part of me."

"Every secret place?" he whispered, his lips brushing against hers.

She shivered. "Yes..."

"Here?" he murmured.

A soft gasp escaped her lips. She closed her eyes, arched her back, lifted her hips to his questing touch.

"Here?" he whispered.

She moaned, trembling, turning into his body, throwing her leg over his thigh, running her hand down his back, stroking his buttocks, moving her hand over his muscular thighs.

"Everywhere," she whispered. "I want you to touch me everywhere, just as I'll touch you...."

Incredibly, he was inside her again, fiercer this time, a savage lover, pressing himself ever deeper, seeking, thirsty, as if she contained the answer he needed to live.

When pleasure overtook her, she felt as if she were drowning in some secret pool of rapture. And Jed was there with her.

Sweat beaded her forehead, moistened her hair. Their chests stuck together from it, moist and hot. A steamy, musky odor enveloped them, the lush scent of sex. Exhausted, she let her arms fall from him, rolled her head to one side.

"My God," she whispered, completely spent.

He rolled off her. He lifted his hand and rubbed his face, turned his head and looked out the window. "The fog's still here. We may be able to do this all day and night."

She rolled onto her side and rubbed his chest. "Let's pray for the fog to stay," she whispered dreamily. "Let's hope it never leaves."

A COUPLE HOURS LATER, they showered. The fog began to lift, drifting away gradually, finally allowing the sun to burn its way through. With the sun came humidity, a warm, muggy air mass that felt like a damp blanket after the previous day's air.

Over lunch, she asked him about his father.

"Dad was a drifter," Jed replied, his face serious as he looked into the past. "My mother died when I was born. He left me with my mother's sister. Concetta. She raised me till I was six, then Dad came back. He took me with him when he left." Jed smiled as the host of memories drifted back. "He gave me my first ball and glove that day he came back, and we went outside Concetta's old place and played catch. He asked me what I wanted to be when I grew up and I said the first thing that came to mind. 'I want to be a major-league pitcher,' I said. He smiled and picked me up in his arms. 'Then that's what you'll be.' "

"Is he still alive?" Con asked softly. She was sitting across from him, watching with eyes that were warm and filled with newfound caring.

"He died five years ago."

"I'm sorry," she said gently. "It must hurt to know he never got to see you pitch in the major leagues."

"I think he does," Jed said, then looked down as if he'd said too much and she might laugh at him.

She didn't laugh. "I believe in angels," she said simply, sharing part of herself just as he'd just done.

He looked up. "You do?"

She nodded. "Sometimes I'll be driving or something and I'll just miss being hit by a car and I'll take a shaky breath and think, 'My guardian angel must be close by.'" She shrugged. "Maybe it's silly, but I believe it."

"It's not silly," he said. "That's why I think Dad sees me. I think he's in heaven, and he knows I made it to the big leagues."

She felt tears spring into her eyes. "I think it's wonderful you believe that. It must feel so good, so comforting."

He nodded. "There aren't any regrets. I don't waste time grieving over Dad not being alive to see me pitch. I know he knows. It's something . . . I don't know . . . I guess it's a form of faith."

She put her elbows on the table and rested her chin on her hands. "This is so nice. This is just about the most perfect weekend of my life."

"It is the most perfect for me," Jed said.

Joy shone in her eyes. She reached out and touched his hand. "I'm happy, Jed."

"Me, too."

"I wish we could stay longer."

"Me, too."

She laughed. "Is that all you can say?"

"Until you stop saying things I agree with."

She sat and looked at his hand holding hers and felt chills travel through her. She lifted her eyes to his. "What's going to happen now?"

"We'll go back to the mainland with Art."

"No, I meant . . . what happens when we go back to Boston?"

"What do you want to happen?"

"I want to start teaching you to read."

"Okay. I want that, too."

"The first thing I want you to do is learn the alphabet."

"Okay, so teach me."

"You'll have to memorize it. The next time I see you, I'll want you to recite it by heart."

"*A, B, C,*" he said, then stopped. "For you, Con, I'll do it."

She shook her head. "No, Jed. For you."

"FOG FINALLY LIFTED," Art said as the ferry pulled away from the dock at Jade Island. "For a while there, I was afraid it wouldn't."

"It lifted here a few hours ago," Jed said.

"Not on the mainland till an hour ago," Art replied. "You two have a good weekend?"

"Fine," Jed said noncommittally.

"Yes, very nice," Con said, smiling formally. She glanced at Jed, who winked at her. She smiled back, feeling relieved. To outsiders, they weren't ready to present themselves as a couple, but alone with each other, they were okay.

"Muggy today," she commented to Art.

"Ayuh," he grunted, his pale blue eyes scanning the horizon. "Jet stream's way up in Canada. This heat's from the south. Be here a few days, they warn. Hot as hell in Boston, I hear." He glanced at Jed. "You pitchin' again soon?"

"Thursday night in Chicago."

Con turned to look at Jed. "When are you leaving?"

"Tuesday morning. We'll be in Chicago and Cincinnati. I'll be back in a week."

"Oh." She stared down at her hands on the ferry's railing. "I won't see you for a while, then."

"Well, I was kind of hoping to see you tonight and tomorrow night."

"Okay," she said, smiling. "I think I can manage that."

"We can continue our lessons. When I get back from the trip, I'll be able to recite the entire alphabet for you."

She hesitated, then said slowly, "If I ever do write that story, Jed, it'd be nice if you could read it."

He studied the coastline they were approaching. "Yes, it would."

"That would make it . . . almost bearable, wouldn't it?"

He narrowed his eyes and scanned the horizon. "It wouldn't matter, then, would it?" he said at last. "I mean, then nothing would matter anymore."

She put her hand on his. "You'll be able to read some day, Jed," she said softly. "I promise."

He turned his head and looked into her eyes. "You make lots of promises, Con. Maybe you should be careful. It could be pretty disappointing, if you find you couldn't keep them all."

"I'll keep them," she vowed.

He didn't respond. He just put his hand over hers and turned his eyes toward the advancing coastline.

Chapter Thirteen

"What do mean, you don't have a story?" Vinnie demanded the next day.

Con shrugged. "Just what I said, Vinnie. I don't have a story."

"You spent the entire weekend with the best pitcher in the country and you don't have a *story?*" her boss yelled. "What's the matter with you, Con? You gone crazy?"

Connie sat at her desk, filing her nails. It wouldn't do any good to yell back at Vinnie. She'd just let him get it out of his system, once and for all.

"I'll tell you what's the matter," Charlie Huff said from the sidelines. "She's gone sweet on the guy."

Connie looked up, a faint flush creeping into her face. "Charlie, this is none of your business."

"Yeah, it is my business, Con," Charlie said, redfaced. "You're in my territory now, honey. You're stepping on my toes here and I don't like it. You found something, didn't you? You found out what he's hiding."

She sighed gustily. "He's not hiding anything, Charlie. The man refused to talk to me. It was the most horrible weekend I've ever spent. I mean, he just wouldn't talk to me."

"Yeah," Charlie said knowingly, "you spent all weekend in bed. He didn't talk, all right, he moaned."

She rolled her eyes and wished her cheeks weren't burning. "You have a gutter mentality, Charlie. I'll bet your dreams are disgusting."

"Okay, okay, you two, break it up," Vinnie said. "Charlie, get lost. I'm talkin' to Con."

"I'll talk to you later," Charlie warned Con, then turned on his downtrodden heel and left.

Vinnie sighed and took a seat next to Con. "Okay, what's going on? You holding something back?"

"Absolutely not."

Vinnie studied her. "You know I warned you, Con. No story, no more chances."

She stopped filing her nails and stared down at them. "I know, Vinnie."

"Well? Your career mean so little you won't even do a story on the charity auction?"

"That's fluff, Vinnie. Is that what you want from me? Fluff?"

"Hey, it's better than nothing. Right now, you're telling me you got no story at all. I don't believe you,

Con. I think Charlie's right. I think you're holding back."

"Sorry, Vinnie, you're wrong."

"You look different, Con. Happier. You sweet on Duval, like Charlie says?"

She rolled her eyes again. "When have I ever been sweet on any man, Vinnie? You know me. I hate men."

"Uh-huh," Vinnie said softly, his eyes speculative. "Well, I guess you're back on society, right, Con?"

"I guess so, Vinnie."

"You upset about that? Sorry you booted your only chance? Feeling anything along those lines?"

"Nope."

"I don't believe you," he said flatly. He leaned forward, his nose an inch away from hers. "You're lying, Con. You're protecting Jed Duval. What's he done, hmm? He in trouble of some kind?"

"Vinnie," she said, exasperated. "I'm not hiding anything. I told you, the man wouldn't talk to me."

"Sure, Con," Vinnie said flatly. "Sure."

She glanced up at her boss. "I'm sorry. I know you're disappointed. I am, too."

"Yeah?" He nodded. "Are you really?"

"Do you think I like being the butt of Charlie Huff's ridicule?" she asked, her cheeks really red now. "You think I like him running around the office jeering at me?"

"Con, if I could prove you were holding out on me, I'd fire you."

"On what grounds?"

"Withholding a story. What're you up to? You think you can sell something to *Time,* the *National Enquirer,* maybe? You'd get a lot more money for it than you would here."

"I told you," she said tiredly. "I'm not holding out on you. I'm not going to write anything on the man. I know diddly squat about the guy. He's a clam, Vinnie. A verifiable clam."

"Okay, I'll have to take you at your word. But I'm warning you, Con—I ever find out you held out on me, I'll have your ass."

"Fine," she said shortly. "It'll be yours if you want it."

Her boss stood up and walked away. He didn't look back. Connie took a shaky breath and sat back. Lord, this was harder than she'd thought it'd be....

THAT NIGHT, JED CAME to her apartment. She had a pad of paper and two pencils waiting on the kitchen table. "Okay," she said when they had taken seats. "This is how you make an *A.*" She printed a capital *A.* "Now you do it."

Awkwardly, Jed tried to duplicate what he saw.

"Good," she said, smiling. "All letters can be written two ways—as capital letters or upper case, like this, some call it the big *A,* and as lower case, the little *a*, like this." She printed a small *a*. "Okay, draw the capital *A*, then the small *a*."

He shook his head, puzzled. "Why two ways?"

"English is a funny language, Jed. It has lots of ways to do things. Capital letters are used at the beginning of certain kinds of words—proper nouns, like a person's name, or at the beginning of a sentence." She searched his eyes and saw that he was still confused. "Don't worry about it yet. You'll understand in time."

"I want to understand now," he protested.

"Trust me," she said. "You'll get it soon." She drew the capital *B,* then a small letter *b*. "Capital *B*," she said, pointing to it. "Small *b*."

Jed stared at the letters. "What's your name look like printed?"

"*C-O-N,*" she said, enunciating each letter as she wrote it.

He stared down at her name. "Con," he said.

She printed *TED*. "Ted," she said. "Ed with a *T* in front of it makes Ted."

"Ted," he repeated, then his face lit up. "Bed?"

"Yes!" She printed it: "Bed, with a *b*."

"Well?" he said, taking her hand. "Do you?"

"Do I what?"

"Want to go to bed?"

She put her arms around him. "Yes," she whispered, her forehead resting against his chest. "Yes, I do...."

CHARLIE HUFF STOOD in the shadows in front of Connie's apartment building, his eyes on the window where only moments ago Jed Duval had pulled down the shade. Two shadows briefly appeared together, then disappeared. Grunting, he threw his cigarette to the sidewalk and ground it under his heel. He took out another cigarette and lit it.

"No story, eh, Con?" he muttered. "We'll see about that...." Turning, he walked off into the darkness.

"YOU CAN'T STAY ALL NIGHT?" Con asked sleepily two hours later.

They had made love, then fallen briefly asleep. Now Jed stood dressing in the middle of the bedroom.

"Sorry, Con, but the plane leaves late tomorrow morning and I still have to pack. I'll call you tomorrow night."

She got up and put her arms around him. "I'll miss you."

"I'll miss you, too. Any chance you could come along?"

"No such luck," she said, smiling wryly. "Vinnie has me back on society. I've got to start pulling my weight."

"What'd he say when you told him you didn't have a story on me?"

"He was angry, but he got over it," she said. She went up on tiptoe and kissed him lingeringly. "Win the next one for me."

He ran his hands up and down her back. "If I even think about you, I'll lose for sure. I'm afraid my concentration's going to be down to zero."

"Then don't think about me," she whispered. "At least not too much."

Grinning, he kissed her, then helped her into her robe.

"I'll walk you to the door," she said, yawning sleepily.

At the door, he took her in his arms and kissed her. She opened her eyes when the kiss ended. "Take care of yourself, Duval," she whispered.

"I'll call you when I get back."

"A week seems like a long time," she said, feeling suddenly nervous. Every woman dreaded a man leaving. It would be a very simple thing for him to return to Boston and never call her again. What would that make her? A big-league loser? Or just an amateur at love?

"Why don't you fly out to Cincinnati this weekend? We could take in the sights."

"After bidding for you at that charity auction, I'm not going to be doing any discretionary spending for quite a while."

"I thought The *Courier* picked up the tab for that."

"They would have if I'd gotten a story," she said. "But I didn't, remember? You cost me five thousand bucks."

"Was I worth it?"

She looked into his eyes. "Every penny of it."

He reached out and caressed her cheek. "Take care, Con."

"You, too."

He was gone then, and she was left with a sinking feeling of abandonment. She wasn't good at trusting, yet the next week would call for a lot of trust on her part. Would he call when he returned to Boston, or would she be forgotten by then, just another baseball groupie he'd managed to fit into a hectic schedule?

She chided herself at her thoughts, realizing that they said a lot more about her self-esteem than they did about her feelings for Jed. If she believed in herself more, she'd have a lot more faith that Jed would call her when he got back to town.

As it was, a niggling feeling of anxiety gnawed at her. For some reason, she was worried that something would go wrong. But what could? She wouldn't write the story about Jed, so nothing could go wrong.

Still, it took her two hours to get to sleep, and when she at last drifted off, a strange feeling of apprehension still nagged at the edges of her consciousness.

SHE WAS HALFWAY to her desk the next morning when she saw Charlie Huff lounging against the wall. She slowed for a fraction of a second, then went right on by.

"Hello to you, too, Kenyon," Charlie said as he fell into step beside her. "Or is it Kennedy?"

She faltered, then kept right on walking. She knew she was in trouble; her heart was suddenly hammering. "Charlie, I'm busy, okay? I don't know what you're trying to do, but it has to wait."

"Something like this can't wait too long," Charlie said in a low, singsong voice. He took a sheaf of papers out of his inside jacket pocket and handed them to her. "Take a look, sweetheart. See if it's familiar."

She unfolded the papers, her heart thumping madly. She stared down at the faded newspaper clipping, obviously copied on a photocopier. "What's this?" she asked impatiently. If she could pretend long enough, she just might survive the next minute or two.

"Honey," Charlie said unctuously, "you're a great little actress, but Streep herself couldn't pull this off." He tapped the article. "Your dad?"

She swallowed. It was here, the moment she'd dreaded for over ten years. She nodded briefly. "Yes," she said. "But I imagine you already knew that."

"I know it all, Con."

She took an unsteady breath and wished there was a window open. She needed fresh air, not this canned stuff they called air-conditioning. "I doubt you know it all, Charlie," she said coolly. "Even I'm not sure I know it all."

"Who woulda thunk it," Charlie said, smiling like a shark. "Our little Con Kenyon, the daughter of a two-bit crook. And look how he ended."

She handed him the article. "You can keep this, Charlie. It's obviously the kind of trash you like to read."

"Hey, you puttin' me down?" he asked, pressing an offended hand to his heart. "Me? Your pal Charlie? Hey, Con, I'll bet there're a lot of people who would like to read this story. I bet our readers would fall all over themselves reading this story, if they knew it was about your dad."

She felt very cold, but very much in control. Sometimes, at night, she used to worry about this kind of thing happening, but now that it was here, she found herself oddly unmoved. "Is that a threat, Charlie?" she asked quietly.

"A threat? From your pal Charlie?"

"You are such scum."

He shook the photocopied article under her nose. "Naw, he was scum, Con. Not me."

"Come to the point, Charlie."

"The point," he snarled, his face only inches from hers, "is this, Connie Kennedy. You've got a story that I want. Now this is dead if you give me that story. You don't? It's all over the papers, and I'll personally hand it to Vinnie myself."

"I told you, Charlie," she said, sighing wearily for effect, "I don't have a story on Duval."

"Sure you do," he said. He grinned and licked his lips. "I saw Duval at your place last night. I'll bet he'd like to read this, too, wouldn't he?"

She felt her heart sink. Why hadn't she told Jed everything, when she had the chance? This was no way to find out, having Charlie Huff reveal it. "I bet he would," she said, but she meant something entirely different from what Charlie thought she meant.

"You don't want him to read it, do you, Con? Or have it plastered on the front pages of the *Courier* for all your society fans to read? Would that complicate your life a little?"

"Only a little," she said shortly. If she could just maintain her cool, maybe she could throw Charlie off the scent long enough for her to talk to Jed in person.

"Sweetheart," Charlie said, brushing her back against the wall, "I want that story."

She looked him straight in the eye and pushed him away. "There is no story."

"You are destroyed," he said, his voice low, his eyes filled with hate. "Hear that, Ms. High Society? You're gone from this city. You will be a laughingstock."

"Charlie, think a minute. That story is about my father, not me. If you want to bring up my background, fine, but it can't hurt me."

"The way I write it will hurt."

"Charlie, I don't know what you're talking about. Just leave me alone."

"You stepped onto my turf," he said, pressing his beefy finger into her breastbone. "And I don't like that, sweetheart. I don't like it at all."

She pushed his finger away. "Don't touch me, Charlie," she warned. "Don't ever touch me again."

He pressed his finger into her again. "I'll touch you all I want," he whispered. "And you won't say a word."

She felt suffocated. The hallway grew dark. Charlie Huff's low voice was muffled. All she could feel was his finger pressed into her. Suddenly everything started whirling around. She felt as if she were on a merry-go-around. From far away, Charlie called her.

"Con?"

She opened her eyes. Vinnie was standing over her. Dozens of faces floated around her. She stared up at them as if she were miles away in some strange subterranean land. "What happened?"

"You fainted, Con," Vinnie said, holding her head. "We've called an ambulance."

"I'm fine, Vinnie," she said, struggling to sit up. "Where's Charlie?"

"He's the one calling the ambulance."

She sat up. Immediately the room spun around. She leaned against Vinnie. "I'm sorry," she whispered.

"It's okay, Con," Vinnie said. "Must be the heat. It's murder out there."

She leaned back against the wall and closed her eyes. If she lived to be one hundred, she'd never get away from it. It would haunt her every day till she died. There was no escaping her past. It followed her no matter where she was. She hated her life, hated the way it had been and the way it was now. There was only one way to deal with it.

"I have a story, Vinnie," she said, her voice coming from a long way away.

"Sure, Con, but first you got to go to the hospital, Okay? They'll check you out, make sure you're okay."

"I'm fine," she said, laughing softly. "Falling must have done me some good. It knocked some sense into me."

"Con, I'm worried about you," Vinnie said. "Here's the ambulance now."

"Vinnie, I've got to talk to you," she said. "I have a story for you, front-page stuff."

"About Duval?"

She almost laughed. Poor Vinnie. He was so hot for a story about Jed Duval. She looked up and saw Charlie Huff staring down at her. She shivered violently.

"You talk to me later, okay, kid?" Vinnie was saying. "Just take it easy now. These nice people are going to put you on the stretcher, take you to the hospital, okay?"

She didn't even answer. That was what she'd do. She'd write the damn story herself. That's what she should have done years ago. Confession. It had been years since she'd taken the sacrament, but she re-

membered how she'd felt afterward, when she was just
a kid, eleven, twelve years old, and she'd just left the
confessional. She'd always felt so clean then, so pure,
so free. Maybe after she told the story, she'd be free
again. Free for the first time in years. . . .

CHARLIE HUFF SPRINTED up the airplane steps and
found his way down the narrow aisle till he spied Duval. "Hey, Jed," he said, taking a seat next to the
pitcher. "How you doin', guy?"

Jed put his head back and closed his eyes. "I don't
talk to reporters, remember?"

"You talk to some reporters," Charlie said. "Connie Kenyon seems to know how to get you to talk."

Jed opened his eyes. "What?"

Charlie grinned. "You were at her place last night,
right? Hey, look, it's okay by me what two adults do
in the privacy of their own homes, but I thought you'd
like to know, she just told Vinnie she's got a front-page
story." Charlie shrugged. "You know what it might be
about?"

Jed turned his head and stared straight ahead. A
muscle worked spasmodically in his cheek. He
clenched his hands into fists. He didn't know what to
do first. He wanted to smash Charlie Huff in the face,
destroy the entire plane, tear it apart piece by piece.
Instead, he put his head back and closed his eyes.

"If there's anything you want to share with me,"
Charlie said in a low voice, "I'll try to see what I can

do for you, Jed. You can't trust a woman. Never could. They'll knife you in the back every time.''

"Shut up, Charlie," Jed said in a quiet voice.

Charlie grinned. "Hey, I hope she was worth it. In the sack, I mean."

Jed clenched his fist, then took a deep breath. "Get off the plane, Charlie," he warned. "Or I'll throw you off it when we're five miles up."

"I ain't goin' nowhere," Charlie said, buckling his seat belt. "Except on the road trip with the team. I'll be on you, Jed, like flies on a cow."

Jed didn't say a word. The worst part of it was he'd begun to trust her. He'd believed she wouldn't write the story. That's what hurt the most....

Chapter Fourteen

Vinnie Carbone looked up from the story. Connie sat in a chair by his desk, staring out the window. It was only a matter of time now. Soon the thing she'd kept secret for so many years would be public property. She felt nothing. She was just enormously tired, exhausted, she suspected, by the years of living with her secret.

"I don't know what to say," Vinnie said at last. "It's a terrific story, Con, but why'd you write it? You could have just gone on pretending. Nobody would have ever known."

"Charlie Huff knows," she said wearily. "He's threatened me he'll write about it, if I don't give him information on Jed Duval."

"Do you have anything on Duval to give him?"

She didn't answer right away. What could she say? Hadn't she realized yet the enormous damage that was done by living a lie?

"I found something out about Duval, Vinnie, but I promised him I wouldn't write anything until he gave me permission."

Vinnie stared at the floor. "What is it? He in trouble with the law, that kind of thing?"

She shook her head. "Nothing like that at all. It's just..." She shrugged helplessly. "It's something he hasn't felt able to cope with. It wouldn't mean much to a lot of people, but to Jed, it's everything." She gestured to the story he held. "Sort of like this, I suppose."

"So that's why you won't write the story," Vinnie said gently. "You don't want to do to Duval what Charlie Huff is threatening to do to you."

She nodded.

"Con, Charlie Huff can write ten of these and we wouldn't publish them. What would be the sense? The way you've written it, you've given it all kinds of heart. It's powerful, coming from you, but from Charlie?" Vinnie shook his head. "We don't need it, Con."

"I don't imagine that would stop him, Vin. He'd just bring it to another paper and they'd publish it."

"And you want to defuse his bomb."

She nodded. She was too tired to speak, too tired to even think properly. She had stayed up all night working on the story. Now she just felt empty, as if everything had drained from her when she put the words on paper.

"You don't know much about Charlie, do you, Con?" Vinnie asked.

"He writes a good sports story."

"Charlie and I broke into the business together, back thirty years ago. He was a lot like you, Con—ambitious, out to make a name for himself, always hungry for a story. There was no Barons franchise then, of course, so he covered the Sox. We had a young girl on the staff. She was pretty and smart and she and Charlie fell in love. Of course, in those days, fraternizing with co-workers was strictly forbidden. But they fell in love, and no rules were going to stop them. Her name was Holly."

Vinnie fell silent, gazing back in his mind's eye to a time thirty years distant, seeing it all, remembering them as they'd been then, he and Charlie Huff and Holly.

"It was harder for a woman in those days, Con. It's still hard now, I suppose, but it's nothing like it was then. And Holly was ambitious too. Hell, we all were.

"Charlie had a great story on an old Red Sox player and of course he shared everything with Holly. One day, while he was still trying to write it—Charlie wasn't as good then as he is now—he opens the *Courier* and finds it all there, under Holly's byline."

Connie stared, pulled in despite herself. "Oh, no."

"Yeah," Vinnie said. "He gets a karate chop to the head by the woman he loves, the one he trusted most on earth."

"I see," she said quietly, and she did.

"Now, Charlie," Vinnie went on, "Charlie reacted the way lots of people do. He got bitter, resentful. He was angry. He carried his rage around in his gut. And it's just gotten worse as time's gone on. He expects to be hurt, Con. He's come to expect that people will stab him in the back and take his story. So he's responded by doing it to others before they can do it to him."

She took a breath and let it out slowly. "You think anything ever turns out right?"

"There's hope, Con," Vinnie said gently.

"I wonder."

"Hey, this story is a start, kid. The truth seems to work most of the time."

"It's funny. At the time, you don't think you're lying. You think you're doing what has to be done. There doesn't even seem to be a choice. You do what you have to do to stay alive."

"Most things are about survival, Con."

"Yes," she said softly, "they are for Jed and me and even Charlie Huff."

Vinnie nodded. "It's a great story, kid, the way you wrote it. Some people would have gone for sensation. You didn't. You went for the heart."

"What else matters?" she asked softly.

"In the end?" Vinnie said. "Nothing."

THAT NIGHT, CONNIE FELL into bed, then realized that Jed hadn't called. Of course, it was Thursday. He had pitched today, yet she hadn't even remembered to turn on the game and watch. And if he'd called last night, as he'd promised he would, she had been at work and wasn't here to receive the call.

She considered finding out where the team was staying and calling him herself, but she was too tired. Exhaustion gripped her. Worn out, she turned on her side and slept.

The next morning, she got a copy of the team's itinerary and called the hotel in Chicago. The Barons had just checked out. She opened the sports page and saw with a sinking heart that Jed had lost his second game.

"It's clear that's something's eating Jed Duval," Charlie Huff had written in his bylined article, "but who knows what? Duval doesn't ever talk to reporters, but right now it appears he isn't even talking to teammates. One thing is sure, the Boston Barons appear to be headed into a nosedive now that ace pitcher Jed Duval has lost two in a row. There's a feeling in the clubhouse that hasn't been there since Duval came up last year and started his amazing ride to fame. Tempers are short. No one's playing practical jokes. No one's even talking, least of all Jed Duval...."

Connie glanced at the Barons' itinerary. They'd be playing in Cincinnati the next three days, then head back to Boston. Frustrated, she threw down the schedule. Jed wouldn't pitch again until the first game in Boston.

She couldn't stop anxiety from eating away at her. Charlie Huff was out there, she was sure, hanging around Jed like an overwhelming shadow. Had Charlie said something to Jed? Had he told him everything? Was that what was bothering Jed? That she hadn't shared everything with him?

She found out the name of the hotel in Cincinnati where the team would stay. Dialing, she left a message at the front desk. When Jed Duval checked in, please have him call her in Boston. It was urgent. Did they understand? Urgent.

"Yes, Ms. Kenyon, I understand," the sweet switchboard operator said.

Connie hung up. She had a sinking sensation in her gut. Something wasn't right. But there was nothing she could do but wait for Jed to call.

HE DIDN'T CALL THAT night, nor did he call the next day. Connie sat at her desk and chewed on her fingernails. The Barons had lost their opening game in Cincinnati, after losing all three games in Chicago. Charlie Huff's articles kept up the nagging: "What's wrong in the Barons' clubhouse? Did everything hinge on Jed Duval's winning every game? If so, the Barons are in trouble. Witness their four lost games in a row so far on this road trip."

Connie threw down the paper and muttered a low curse at Charlie Huff. She might understand him better, but she still didn't like him. She could imagine the pressure Jed must be under right now, having just lost two games in a row and watching his team slide out of first place.

She placed another call to the hotel in Cincinnati.

"I'm sorry, Ms. Kenyon, but we've given him his messages."

"Well, give him another," Connie said. "Tell him I absolutely must talk to him. It's extremely important."

"It's no longer urgent?" the nasal-voiced operator asked cattily.

"Yes, it's urgent!" Connie snapped. "Write it down in red and underline it. Urgent. Is that clear?"

"Yes, Ms. Kenyon." The operator's nasal voice was decidedly cool now.

Con hung up, feeling impotent. She rubbed the aching muscles in the back of her neck and shoulders, then slid down lower in her chair. Sunday's paper would carry her story. She felt nothing, not even relief. She was just tired. More than anything, she needed to get away and have a rest. She laughed to herself sardonically. Strange, she'd just come back last weekend from Jade Island. Why did the effects of vacations never seem to last more than a day?

She finished up her work and left for the day. Maybe Jed would call tonight. She'd wait by the phone till midnight if she had to. She couldn't stand not hearing from him, couldn't stand the anxiety that wormed around in her stomach. If Charlie Huff had said something to Jed, she'd personally take off Charlie's head at the shoulders....

ON SATURDAY, CONNIE kept herself busy doing errands, cleaning till her place sparkled. She didn't think; she worked. On Saturday night, exhausted, she fell into bed and waited for the phone to ring. It didn't.

On Sunday, she got up and retrieved the paper from the hallway outside her door. Feeling sick to her stomach, she sat down and began to read:

Ellsworth Street in Meecham, Massachusetts is a lonely place. Hope deserted it years ago, along with Jerry's Hardware Store, the Freeze 'n' Breeze ice-cream parlor and Sno-Flake Dry Cleaners. A few businesses still struggle for existence, like the grass that grows in the cracks of the cement sidewalks. What remains is desolation and empty boarded-up buildings.

Out on Route 128, great glass buildings gleam in the sun, the homes of high-tech industry, real-estate developers, office parkades. On Ellsworth Street, it is perpetually gloomy. The windows don't shine here, nor do the inhabitants. They struggle to make a living, working in Mc-Donald's or Burger King, shopping at K-Mart, dreaming of one day making it big.

One former inhabitant of Ellsworth Street did make it big, but she did it by weaving a life based on lies, by turning her back on Ellsworth Street and her past. This is my story. None of the names have been changed to protect the innocent. Sometimes I don't think anyone was innocent. Other times, I think we all were....

She skipped down the page to the section near the end. This was the hardest part, telling about what had happened that terrible afternoon when her father was killed. She didn't know if she saw the words on the page or the images in her memory. The two seemed to blur, so that as she read the words, she saw again the fateful events leading to that last fatal encounter.

After her mother left, her father lost all hope. It was as if her leaving was the final blow that sent him over the edge into full despair. He had always taken a few drinks; he'd said it helped him face each day. Now he began to drink more, harder. Whole weekends were lost. He began to stay out of work. Eventually he lost his job.

She remembered that, for her, fear was constant, never-ending. She was afraid they would lose their house. Her father went on unemployment. He scrambled for work in the neighborhood, mowing a scraggly lawn here and painting a house there. They got by. Schoolwork was her only defense against the complete disintegration of her life. She stayed in her room and studied, as if by closing her eyes to reality she might actually be able to change it.

They lived in the same house, yet had nothing to say to each other. They coexisted. Then his unemployment benefits ran out. She remembered entering the kitchen one day and finding him at the table staring into space. She remembered the hatred for him.

"You're not my father," she yelled in a contemptuous voice. "You're weak! I hate you! I hate you!"

And she turned and raced from the house, running until it felt as if her lungs might burst. She had cried until there were no more tears left.

But where could she go? She was seventeen years old. She wanted to finish her high-school education. She wanted to go to college. Education was her way out. So she went home.

And she did it. She went to school, got the best grades in class and won a full scholarship to Smith.

She didn't examine her father's life too closely. She didn't ask where the money came from that payed the bills. She didn't speak to him. She did what she had to do because this was about survival, her survival.

And then one day the police knocked on the door and told her. Her father was in the hospital. He had been shot in an attempted robbery. Would she like to go to the hospital to see him?

As she stood and watched him, his eyes flickered open. He moistened his lips with his tongue. His fingers fluttered helplessly. Without even realizing it, she reached out and took his hand. "Hello, Daddy."

He looked up at her. Tears swam in those sorrowful pale eyes. "I'm sorry, Con. I shouldn't have done it."

She made a noise, inarticulate. She couldn't speak. What could she say if she could?

"I'm sorry," he repeated. "I made a mess of my life, but you're going to do fine, Con. You're the smart one in the family. You'll make something of yourself. You're not like me."

She felt a terrible lump form in her throat, a sad and sorrowful buildup of love and confusion and remorse and anger. She couldn't comprehend it all, couldn't bring all the disparate feelings together to make sense of them. They overwhelmed her, swamped her the way a flooding river swamps the banks that normally contain it.

A tear fell from her eyes, but she was conscious only of this terrible, overwhelming mixture of pain and incomprehension. She who needed to understand things, who liked to master facts and recite them back on exams and tests, couldn't understand any of this. All she knew was that something welled up inside her that she hadn't even known was there, some overwhelming need to make things right, to change everything, to once and for all clear the slate.

"I love you, Daddy," she whispered, squeezing his hand. "I love you."

And he had smiled, and in his eyes she saw the one thing she'd never seen there before, the one thing that had seemed to evade him all his life. She saw hope.

And then he died.

"I'm sorry, Daddy," she whispered, but he was gone. It was her everlasting penance, to know he hadn't heard those words.

She sat in her living room and felt the lump back in her throat. Then she lowered her gaze and read the last of the article.

Ellsworth Street in Meecham, Massachusetts is a lonely place. The people who live there no longer see the sun, even when it shines. Dragged down by poverty, they live on the fringes of society. Route 128 with its gleaming glass towers may be only a couple of miles away, but to the people of Ellsworth Street in Meecham, it's more like a thousand miles. On Meecham Street, there is no hope, and that is the greatest tragedy of all.

Con lifted her head and realized that tears were falling down her cheeks. She brushed them away but they kept falling, gentle, quiet tears that seemed endless, from some bounteous spring of sadness located deep within her soul.

Chapter Fifteen

She had written the society column for the *Boston Courier* for three years. In that time, she'd always been greeted warmly, bussed on the cheek, had her hand held, squeezed. She'd been treated to dinner, to drinks and almost everything in between.

Today, Boston society cut her dead. Not a face smiled. No one at the fashion show came up to her, called out her name, reached for her hand. One or two women at the Ritz-Carlton almost met her eyes but looked away quickly. An elderly woman smiled falsely, then hurried out the door.

In the ladies' room, she overheard a group of women whispering about her.

"It's shocking!" one murmured under her breath. "I was stunned."

"Who would have ever *thought?*" gasped another.

"I'll never be able to see her again without thinking of that horrible story. Why would she ever write it?"

"I always knew she was low-class," another claimed haughtily. "You can tell. She doesn't wear her clothes right."

In her stall, Con arched a wry brow and apologized silently to Anne Klein and Ralph Lauren. Squaring her shoulders, she opened the door. The group of women fell silent. Hurriedly, they scurried from the ladies' room. Only one woman couldn't escape—her hands were wet.

"Hello, Sheila," Con said.

Sheila Henry blanched. "Con."

"Lovely day," Con said, smiling. "The clothes are fabulous."

"Yes."

"Was that your little girl, Melissa, modeling that black velvet dress?"

"Yes." Sheila Henry dried her hands and turned her back and left without another word.

Con sighed. So much for truth telling. Maybe she should have just kept it to herself. But, then, if this was the reaction she got from writing her own story, what would have happened if Charlie Huff had written it? They'd probably have ridden her out of town on a rail to Salem and burned her at the stake.

She went back to work and wrote a story about the fashion show. She submitted it to Vinnie. He tossed it in his basket. "How you doing?"

She shrugged. "Two hate calls and complete ostracism at the fashion show. Other than that, I'm fine."

"You having regrets now?"

She debated. "What else could I do? Leave the fodder for Charlie Huff to use as he chose?"

"You'll be okay, Con. These things die down after a few weeks. In a month or two, the social lions will be smiling on you again."

"A month?" she echoed. "By that time, I may die from the icy glances I'm getting."

"Keep joking, Con. Humor helps."

"Sure," she said. "So does anesthesia when you're being cut open."

"Charlie's back," Vinnie said.

"Oh, Lord." She sat down. "I can take all the other stuff. This, I don't know if I can handle." She glanced at Vinnie. "He see the story?"

"I presume so."

"He say anything?"

"Nope."

"He'll be furious."

"Those are the breaks."

"He'll also be on me about Jed's story."

"What about Jed's story, Con?" Vinnie frowned. "I told you if I ever found out you'd held something back, I'd fire you."

Connie felt her stomach drop out. Please, not anything else. She couldn't handle anything else right now. She needed her job. It allowed her to do silly, inconsequential things such as pay her bills.

"Vinnie, I'm not going to write it till I get Jed's permission, but I will, I promise you. He just needs some time to deal with things."

"Con, look, I know you're going through a difficult time right now, but this is a business. We don't have time for personal problems, okay? We've got deadlines here. I let you get away with this, others will try."

"Others don't have to know."

"Con, it's the principle."

"Principle, hell!" she snapped. "I've got principles, too, Vinnie, and I'm not going to violate them."

"Okay, so maybe you better start looking for another job."

She stared at him. "You're kidding. You've got to be kidding."

But when she looked into Vinnie's eyes, she knew he wasn't.

THERE WAS NO MESSAGE on her telephone answering machine from Jed when she got home. There was no message from anyone.

She decided to take the bull by the horns and call him. She dialed the private number and his answering machine came on: "I'm unable to answer the phone right now. Please leave a message at the tone."

She waited for the tone, then said, "Jed? It's Con. I..." She stared at the floor, frozen. What could she say? "Call me, please."

A moment after she hung up, the phone rang. Joy shot through her. It was Jed; it had to be.

"Hello, Con."

Her heart fell. It wasn't Jed; it was Charlie Huff.

"Hello, Charlie."

"I've got to hand it to you. You outsmarted me. But I'll find a way to get even. Believe me, Con, this isn't over between us."

THE NEXT DAY, CON WENT to Barons Field. When Jed saw her, he turned his back and walked away. She hurried after him. "Jed, what's wrong?"

He didn't answer.

She tugged at his arm. "Jed, dammit, talk to me."

He looked at her with cold, angry eyes. "I don't talk to reporters, Ms. Kenyon."

"I didn't write it, Jed."

"Charlie says you already have. He said you told your editor you had a front-page story for him about me."

"And you believe Charlie over me?"

"That's right."

She stared at the man she thought she loved, then realized she was a fool. "It's too bad you can't read,

Duval," she said in an angry voice. "Then you'd see for yourself what story I wrote."

"I guess that's not going to happen, is it?" he snapped.

"Why? Are you going to give up?"

"Who cares? Once your story hits the paper, it won't matter if I can read or not. Everyone will know."

"It would still matter whether you can read," she said. She was shaking she was so angry. She wished she could shake Duval.

"Get out of my way, Con," he said in a cold voice. "Get out and stay out."

"I didn't write that story, Duval, and I'm not going to write it. Not till you give me permission."

"That'll be a frigid day in hell," he said, and turned on his heel and walked away.

She stared at him, wishing she could go after him, knowing she couldn't. He couldn't believe her. Whatever had happened in his past had convinced him that reporters couldn't be trusted. It was the supreme irony that when he at last chose to trust one, he chose Charlie Huff, the least trustworthy of all.

A WEEK LATER, CON HANDED her letter of resignation to Vinnie. "I'm going back to Meecham," she said.

"Meecham?" He stared at her. "What are you? Crazy?"

"No doubt. But there's a little paper there, the *Meecham Times,* and they need a reporter. The editor contacted me. He read my story in the *Courier.* He said it's exactly the kind of thing he wants his paper to do all the time. He promised me complete carte blanche. I'm going to do investigative stuff, social commentary he calls it."

"How much you making?" Vinnie asked wryly.

"Not much." She shrugged. "Enough to get by."

"You're a fool, Con. Write the story on Duval and I'll give you a five-thousand-dollar raise and the same opportunity you're getting on the *Meecham Times,* but with fifty times the circulation."

"I'm sorry, Vinnie. If you had allowed me to do what I felt was right, I'd have stayed here. You wouldn't do that, though. You told me to pack and leave. Fine, I'm leaving. I won't be coming back."

"Your career's dead," he predicted.

"Maybe, maybe not. All I know is, I can sleep at night."

"All your high and mighty principles," he said softly.

"Someone's gotta have 'em," she said. "Especially around this place." Turning, she walked out.

Chapter Sixteen

"You see that article by Connie Kenyon in last Sunday's paper?" Randy Carter asked Jed as they suited up in the locker room.

Jed went very still. "What story?"

"She wrote a story about herself. Amazing. I couldn't believe it when I read it. It seems she's not the rich bitch she looks like. She came from a real poor family in some little two-bit town called Meecham, and it turns out her father was a small-time hood. Got killed by the cops in a holdup. Can you beat that? Her name isn't even Kenyon. It's Kennedy." Randy shook his head. "Just goes to show—you can't judge a book by its cover."

Jed stared into his locker, unmoving. "No," he finally said. "I didn't see it. Do you still have the article?"

"Unless the wife threw it out."

"Could you bring it in to me, if you still have it?" Jed asked.

"Sure." Randy eyed him speculatively. "Why? You got a thing going with her?"

"No."

Randy shrugged. "Wouldn't blame you if you did. Nice-looking gal."

Jed almost laughed to himself. What would he do with the article if he got it? He couldn't read the damn thing. What did he think would happen? Would the words somehow find a way into his brain and suddenly enlighten him about Con?

He felt discouraged and disappointed. He didn't know what was wrong with him. He wasn't even enjoying baseball lately. It was more than just losing his last two games. It was more a general sense of dissatisfaction. In small ways, he was feeling tired, irritable. Something was missing, but he couldn't put his finger on it. Was it baseball? Or was it him?

"Haven't seen Con hanging around you much lately," the catcher, Larry Connors, said as they walked up the long, dark runway toward the brightness that was Barons Field.

"No," Jed said heavily. "I expect she got tired of my not talking to her."

"Why is that, Jed?" Larry asked. "Why won't you talk to reporters?"

They had reached the end of the runway and were standing in the opening that led onto the field. The sun was high and bright in a cloudless sky. Players were scattered on the field, jogging, taking catch, shagging flies in batting practice.

Jed stood there and wondered how to answer Larry. He wasn't even sure he knew the truth any more. What had it all been about, his refusal to talk to reporters? He knew that five years ago he'd promised himself he never would talk to reporters, but now he wondered if it wasn't time to reassess that vow.

"You know, Larry," he said now. "I'm not sure I even know anymore. It's just something I thought was real important once. Now, I'm not sure what's important and what isn't."

Larry nodded. "Well, life's like that, I guess. What mattered most on earth one time ain't worth diddley a few years later." He put on his cap and jogged onto the field.

Jed stood staring after him. Larry wasn't known for his intelligence, but sometimes he made a lot of sense.

CON BOUGHT A TICKET for her usual seat at Barons Field. Already, the fans were filing into the park, stopping to buy hot dogs and beer at the refreshment stands, then strolling to their seats as the loudspeaker blared out the latest Paula Abdul tune.

She made her way to her seat and took her binoculars out of their case. She focused them on Jed. He was out in the bull pen, warming up. He was pitching tonight, and she was nervous. He'd lost his last two games. Would he regain his form tonight, or continue on his downward course?

She couldn't tell from his face. As usual, it was impassive and unemotional. The black paint was daubed under his eyes, his hat was pulled low over his forehead. He held the ball hidden in his glove, both hands at chest level, then went into his stretch, reared back, kicked up his leg and hurled the ball. It sped towards the catcher in the bull pen, a blur of white. She could almost hear it hit the catcher's mitt. WHUP! Like a guided missile coming in for a crash landing.

She remembered Buzz Drummond saying that Larry Connors had told him his hands ached for days after catching Jed in a game. Watching Jed now, she realized that she wasn't concentrating on his body, magnificent as it was. She didn't care about his physique, his strength, his muscles and sinews. She only cared about Jed, the person, the man beneath the bones.

She wished she had the right to go out there and talk to him, to urge him on, to tell him not to worry, he could win again. Then she realized how sad that was, what a foolish dream, to want to be the woman who urged Jed Duval on, helped him realize his dreams. It had more to do with herself than with Jed. She wanted to be important to him, not for him but for herself. She wanted the egotistical payoff of being the woman Jed turned to for succor and support.

If Jed needed someone, he'd have to make the first move. Right now, he was disgusted with her. Charlie

Huff had poisoned his mind against her. All she could do was wait it out, hoping that as the weeks went by and his story never appeared in the papers, he'd at least begin to realize she hadn't betrayed him.

She felt angry, but impotent. Talking to him hadn't worked; he hadn't listened. In his own way Jed was as stubborn as she.

Con sat back to enjoy the game, but it was anything but enjoyable. Jed came out to pitch and everything went wrong. His delivery was uncertain, his ball wild. He threw everything but strikes. The ball hit the dirt three feet in front of the plate, two feet past the plate and everywhere else but where it should have.

He gave up a home run, a towering shot that she knew was out the second it left the bat. The next inning he gave up two runs and with a runner on second, the manager came out of the dugout, signaling for a right-hander.

Jed stood on the mound, impassive, unmoving. He handed the manager the baseball and walked off the mound.

The fans began to boo. Con shifted uncomfortably in her seat. She couldn't believe how the fans had turned on the man who'd been their idol only a couple of weeks ago. She remembered something Jed had said when she first met him, something about not wanting to be a hero. She understood that now.

Sitting in the stands, she felt her heart go out to Jed, not in pity but in understanding. She wished she could stand up and tell all the fans to be quiet, to stop it. She wanted to protect Jed from them, to wrap her arms around him and tell him it was okay, he didn't have to perform to earn her love. He was fine just the way he was, if he won or lost, failed or succeeded.

Tears welled in her eyes, but she dashed them away. Tears wouldn't help Jed. He wouldn't even see them; he was too busy being angry with her. Charlie Huff had made sure of that.

She simply rose from her seat and left the ball park.

THE NEXT DAY, Randy Carter brought Con's article into Jed.

"Thanks, Randy." Jed took it, staring down at the jumbled mass of letters that meant nothing to him. He knew that those letters could magically be unscrambled, that he could learn to decipher their hidden meaning if he learned the secrets of how words were put together. Could he learn to read? Con had said he could if he tried. He had begun to make a start, then Charlie Huff had smashed his world and he'd given up.

He was stuffing the article into his locker when Charlie himself appeared at his side.

"So you read it, eh?" Charlie said, chuckling. "Quite a shocker wasn't it? Who'd've thought our little Con was the daughter of a small-time crook?"

"Actually, I haven't had time to read it yet," Jed said. "What's that about Con's father?"

"Yeah, can you beat it? Turns out she lived in a divey town called Meecham, up near Marblehead. And here she was posing as Ms. Society Dame all these years. Just goes to show, you can't trust anybody, least of all a woman."

"Last week on the plane, you told me she was writing a story about me. Except it's not about me; it's about her."

"She fooled me," he said, shrugging. He leaned a beefy shoulder against Jed's locker and aimed a finger at his chest. "Same as you."

"What are you talking about, Charlie?"

"Jed, I can smell a story around you the way I smell fish at a fish market. Con claims there is no story, but I'm convinced there is. Since she's not gonna spill the beans, why don't you? Maybe we can turn it into a book. There's big money in sports books, Jed. Look at Jim Bouton, Sparky Lyle. Those guys cleaned up on their stories. The fans want to know about you, Jed. If you got something to hide, it's going to come out sooner or later, so why not come clean with me and I'll see to it you get every break that's comin' to you. I'll write the book for you. It'll be a winner, and we can both profit."

"Let me get this straight," Jed said quietly. "Last week you told me Con was writing a story about me, but now it turns out she says she hasn't got a story on me? Which is it, Charlie? Did she tell you she had a story or didn't she?"

"Hey," Charlie said, grinning, "I thought it would work if I told you she said that. You know, Jed, it's an old cardshark trick—smoking out someone's hand. So it didn't work. So what? I ain't lost nothin' and neither have you. You were smart not to let on to Connie. She's a gold digger. If she knew what you're hiding, believe me, it'd be on the front pages like that." He snapped his fingers. "Now me? I'll treat you right, Jed. Take care of you. Protect you from the sharks."

"Charlie," Jed said contemptuously, "you are the sharks." Taking the article from his locker, he turned and walked out of the club house.

Charlie just smiled.

CON WAS PACKING when the doorbell rang that night. She groaned and wiped the sweat from her forehead. She flexed her shoulder muscles and made her way to the door. She found herself face-to-face with Jed.

"Can I come in?" His eyes traveled down her body, taking in the faded jeans that clung to her long legs and the red plaid cotton shirt she wore.

"Sure," she said, standing back and opening the door wide. "By all means. To what do I owe the honor of your presence? You here to rake me over some more coals, Jed? Did Charlie Huff convince you I was the first cousin of Genghis Khan?"

Without speaking, Jed held out the article. "I'd like you to read me this."

She stared down at it, feeling sick inside. "I wondered if you'd heard about it." She sighed and rubbed her forehead. "I suppose Charlie or someone equally nice filled you in on the details."

"Randy Carter told me the high points."

She looked away. "I'm sorry, Jed. I should have told you everything when we were on Jade Island. I don't know why I didn't. I guess I just..." She shrugged. "I was ashamed."

"Just read me the article, would you, please?" he said in a gentle voice.

She took the article from him and gestured for him to sit down on the couch. She sat down across from him. "I don't have to read it," she said. "I know the damn thing word-for-word. I wrote it, after all."

"I'd appreciate it if you'd read it."

"Whatever you say." She held up the newspaper and took a deep breath. She felt suddenly nervous, her hands were sweaty and her voice seemed to be shaking. She took another calming breath and started reading: *"Ellsworth Street in Meecham, Massachusetts is a lonely place. Hope deserted it years ago, along with..."*

She read the entire story, not stopping for breath, and when she had read the last sentence, she didn't look up.

"Why didn't you tell me?" Jed asked softly.

"Why are you afraid to let anyone know you can't read?" she asked just as softly. Her eyes were filled with sadness when she looked at him, but she smiled. "We are two of a kind, Jed."

He sat with his shoulders slumping, his large frame looking tired, worn out. He stared at the floor, then lifted his eyes to hers. "My dad could have died like that, too," he said. "He was lucky, though. He never got caught."

Jed frowned as he remembered his youth. "We'd pack up and move on every few weeks. When my father couldn't get a job as a short-order cook, or in a gas station, he'd take a can of beans from a store shelf, or a pint of milk. I was ashamed of him and by the time I was a teenager, I didn't want to be with him. But I had no choice."

"You never thought of telling him how you felt?" Con asked.

Jed laughed cynically. "We didn't talk much by then. About the only thing we did was play ball. He'd want me to pitch, so he could hit. He loved baseball. Sometimes I think it's the only thing we ever shared."

"Could he read?" she asked.

"Yeah, he could."

"Did you ever tell him you couldn't?"

"What good would it have done?" He shook his head. "He wouldn't have changed. But he fed me and clothed me and he taught me to play ball. He gave me that."

"Too bad he couldn't have given you what you needed," she said bitterly.

"He thought he did," Jed said. "To him, baseball was everything in the world."

She stared at him, feeling angry for him, angry that he didn't even realize all he'd lost out on. "Well, it's clear neither one of us got the best start in life, but at least I knew enough to get an education. You didn't even have the chance to get that. Don't you think it's about time you did?"

"Are you still willing to teach me to read?"

She steeled herself. "I'm afraid I won't be around, Jed. I'm leaving."

Chapter Seventeen

Jed looked around, as if noticing the packing boxes for the first time. "What do you mean, leaving? Where are you going?"

"I'm leaving Boston," she said.

"Why?"

"I took another job at another paper."

"Why, Con? I thought you loved it at the *Courier*."

"Doing the society column got to be boring, Jed. I'm moving back home. There's a small paper there that will let me write what I want without hassling me all the time."

"That's your choice?" Jed asked. "I mean, you didn't have to leave?"

"Of course, I didn't!" she said, acting offended at the suggestion. "That story was a front-page feature, Jed. No one's going to ask a reporter to leave who has a front-page story."

"It just doesn't make sense to me. It'd be like me leaving to go back to the minor leagues."

"It's not the same thing at all," she said haughtily. She refused to let Jed know that Vinnie had asked her to leave because she wouldn't write the story about him. If he hadn't been able to believe her before, she wasn't going to try to make herself sound better to him. From now on, she didn't want to have anything to do with Jed Duval in a personal way. If he couldn't believe in her from the very start, she didn't want him anyway.

"Charlie Huff admitted that you hadn't told him you were doing a story on me."

She felt her heart jump, but she kept cool. "Did he?" she asked vaguely.

"I guess you've got a right to be pretty sore at me."

"I sure do," she agreed.

"Who's to say that you won't write the story at this other paper you're going to work at?"

She felt heart turn over, but refused to show how hurt she was. She glanced at him coolly. "That's right," she said. "And I'm glad you're aware of it. I could write that story any time I wanted to."

He looked into her eyes. She didn't flinch. She was damned if she was going to get on her knees and beg him to believe her. The hell with him. She didn't need him to believe her. He could rot in hell for all she cared.

"But you promised me once that you wouldn't write it unless I gave you permission to."

"Yes, and then you told me you didn't believe me. You told me Charlie Huff had said I was going to write it. If you want to believe Charlie Huff before me, Jed, that's your prerogative."

"Damn it, Con, I can't help it. You've got to realize how hard it is for me to trust reporters."

"You trust Charlie Huff," she said shortly.

"He's never given me any reason to doubt him in the time I've known him."

"Neither have I," she snapped. "But that doesn't seem to hold any water with you."

"All right, I'll admit you have a right to be angry, but I've got reasons why I don't trust reporters."

"Well, I don't know your reasons, Jed. It could be just plain old cussed stupidity on your part, for all I know."

"A reporter ruined the life of a friend of mine," Jed said harshly.

Con stared at him, her anger draining away. "What happened?"

"His name was Philip Turner—everyone called him Flip. He was my best friend in the minors, a talented guy, lots of fun. He had a wife and son who meant everything to him." Jed smiled as he remembered. "He used to read the papers to me when no one was around. He was the only one I ever told I couldn't read—before you."

Con felt the emotion in Jed's voice and she prompted him to continue.

"Flip had a problem with one of the women who hung around the parks—Wanda Jean, I'll never forget her name. She just wouldn't leave him alone, and one night she turned up in his hotel room stark naked." Jed shook his head, as if to shake away the memory. "Flip threw her out and Wanda Jean just screamed at him, saying one day she'd get him for this. And she did."

Jed looked straight at Con, his eyes boring into hers. "She went to a local reporter and told him Flip was throwing games. And that reporter printed it. Didn't even bother to check out her story. When it hit, Flip was banned from baseball and his wife took his kid and left him."

Con knew he placed all the blame on the reporter. She didn't need Jed to spell it out for her. She could feel his pain. "Did they ever get back together? What happened to him?"

"Flip started drinking heavily—he just couldn't handle losing his boy. One night he convinced his wife to go see Wanda Jean, to hear the truth..." He fell silent for a moment. "They never made it. He was drunk. They crashed and they were killed."

"Oh, Jed." Con's hand covered her mouth. She felt sick, as if she'd known Flip herself. "What happened to the boy?"

"He was asleep at home, thank God. But there was no family for him and he ended up in an orphanage. That's why I donate time and money to any orphans' fund. It seems the least I can do for Flip."

"That's horrible, Jed—"

"No, what's horrible is that the reporter never printed the truth. Not even after Wanda Jean confessed that she made up the whole story." The rage was clearly written all over Jed's face. "The bastard refused to print it. Until I got to him."

A shiver went up Con's spine. "What did you do?"

"I made him write it. But he never got what was coming to him. The paper ran the story with a bunch of apologies and then made him sports editor." Jed smiled bitterly. "They rewarded him, for God's sake!"

"No wonder you hate us," Con said softly. "It makes sense now. But, Jed, you've got to know not every reporter is like that."

"All I know is he and his ambition cost me a friend." He moved toward Con, his hand outstretched. His face seemed to soften. "I thought one day maybe Flip would teach me to read. Now he's gone. But you're here," he said, touching her cheek with a tentative finger.

She knew he was going to make a move on her and she knew she couldn't let herself respond to him. Not now, after the way he'd acted toward her, believing Charlie over her. That had put a gap between them, a gap she didn't know could be bridged.

"Look," she said, pulling back from his touch, "I don't think this is going to work. I'm in the middle of moving, and teaching someone to read is harder than you think. Maybe you should get someone else to help you."

"You mean you're backing out on your promise?" he said bitterly.

She felt as if she'd been socked in the stomach. "Jed, there are people who are trained to teach you. People with all kinds of time, and the skills necessary to help you." She lifted her hands and gestured around. "Right now, I'm swamped with my own problems."

"I see," he said.

She felt her heart turn over in her breast. He looked absolutely woebegone, as if his only friend in the world had deserted him, but what could she do? She didn't know how to teach him to read. She was in over her head. Someone else could do it in half the time and much more easily than she could. She had to do this, even if it seemed to Jed that she was deserting him.

"Look, Jed," she said gently, "I'd love to be able to teach you to read, but I don't know how. I really don't, Jed, but there are others who do."

"Forget it," he said, standing up abruptly. "I didn't want to learn anyway."

Anger ripped through her, like a fast-moving storm. "That's right," she said hotly, "take the easy way out, Jed. If you can't do this with me, don't do it at all.

Make sure you make me feel guilty and rotten and mean, because you're the victim, aren't you? Poor Jed Duval. He can't read, and mean old, rotten Con Kenyon won't teach him.''

"All right," he said, "I can see the kind of friend you are. You promise something and then go back on your promise."

She steeled herself to the undeserved slap and nodded. "That's right, Jed. I'm a rotten friend. Now get the hell out and don't bother to come back. I won't be here anyway."

He stared at her, a muscle moving agitatedly in his cheek. "Fine," he said. "Good riddance to you, too."

She stared at him, feeling rotten. Perhaps she could learn how to teach him to read. She'd have time, once she was moved into her new place. But, dammit, she couldn't always be there for Jed, nursing him along like a wet nurse. If she tutored him, he'd always feel he owed it to her. He needed to see that he could learn on his own.

"Sorry, Jed. I don't have time. If you want to learn to read, you'll have to do it yourself."

He stared at her as if he couldn't quite believe she'd said that, then turned and left, slamming the door after him.

She leaned against the door and closed her eyes. "Please God," she prayed, "let him understand. This is something he has to do for himself. I can't do it for him. Please, let him understand. . . .''

Chapter Eighteen

Vinnie Carbone sat at his desk, frowning thoughtfully. He picked up his phone and dialed Charlie Huff's extension. "It's Vinnie. You wanna come in here a minute?"

When Charlie showed up, Vinnie gestured for him to take a seat. "Con left the paper."

"What?" Charlie sat up straighter. This was news. "Why?"

"I asked her to," Vinnie said. "It turns out she was holding out on us. She's got some sort of story on Duval, but she won't write it without his permission."

"Didn't I tell you?" Charlie shouted, his face getting redder by the minute. "The guy's got her hooked."

"Well, now we know there's a story. And I want you to get it, Charlie. Write it before she does."

"That's all I ever wanted," Charlie said.

"Then get it. No excuses, Charlie. I don't care if Duval won't talk to reporters. Make him talk. Hire a private detective if you have to, to scout around his past. Money's no object. I want that story."

"You got it, Vinnie," Charlie said, easing out of his chair. "Believe me, you got it."

Vinnie smiled and watched as Charlie left his office. This is what he liked—the race to the story, pitting one reporter against the other. And it didn't hurt any that the reporter who was going to lose was Con Kenyon. She'd brought it on herself. He sat back and laced his fingers placidly across his stomach. The thought of bringing Con Kenyon down felt so good, he just might treat himself to a three-course dinner from Luigi's.

JED SAT IN FRONT of his locker, staring into space. It had been a week since he'd left Con's, and during that time he'd lost another game. Tomorrow he was set to pitch again, yet he knew he wasn't ready. His mind was in turmoil. He couldn't think straight, couldn't concentrate, couldn't even sleep at night. He kept remembering Con's face when she told him she didn't have time to teach him to read.

There was something about it, something that gnawed at him, but he couldn't quite figure out what it was. She had looked utterly miserable, as if what she was saying was even harder for her than it was for him.

But that was ridiculous. Con was an ambitious career woman. She didn't have time for him now. She was already thinking about her new job, about making a name for herself. If she had truly cared about him, she would have made the time to help him.

But something nagged at him, niggled at the far edges of his consciousness.

"Why should she?" a small voice said. *"Is it her job to take care of you?"*

He didn't want to hear the nagging question, didn't want to have to face the implications. Was that what he wanted from Con? For her to take care of him? He stared at the floor, lost in thought, bogged down in these confusing questions and doubts. He'd never felt this way before about anyone. Women had always been nonessential. They were pleasant diversions after a game, but they had never figured very prominently in his life.

Only baseball had mattered, learning to pitch, getting to the big leagues, becoming a star, making a name for himself. He remembered Con's anger when he'd suggested that a career was important only for a man.

"I can't believe you said that," she'd said, telling him that women cared too, they too wanted to make a name for themselves, had ambitions.

He sat and struggled with his conflicting feelings. Dammit, he wanted a woman to live for *him,* not some lousy job! He wanted her to be there for him at all times, smoothing his way, making him feel special, pampered, loved. He wanted her to put him first and herself second. As far as he went, his job came first. If there was any leftover energy, then of course she'd get it.

Then it hit him, with all the force of a prize-fighter's right jab: *Maybe that's what women wanted too.*

He lifted his eyes and stared into space, dumbfounded by this sudden realization that had come out of nowhere, leaving him dazed. For the first time in his life, he tried to see life from another person's perspective, not just his own. He sat and frowned as he tried to picture what Con's life was like.

She worked hard, he knew that for a fact. She was very serious about her work. She cared.

He felt like shaking his head to clear it from all the fuzz that was clouding his thinking. She cared about her work, she took it seriously—yet she hadn't written that story about him. He sat trying to puzzle it out. It didn't make sense. Something didn't add up. Somewhere along the line, part of the puzzle was missing. Or maybe he was just looking at it wrong.

He was angry that Con didn't have time to teach him to read. He was angry that she said she was too busy, that her job mattered more than he did. Yet when she had the chance to write a potentially big story about him, she hadn't taken it.

Why?

He was staring at nothing, unable to see anything clearly, when he heard Charlie Huff's loud voice from nearby. Shaking off his thoughts, he turned and looked at him.

Charlie Huff was fat. He had a smelly cigar clamped between his teeth. He was laughing at an off-color joke, slapping the ball player who'd told it on the back, his beady eyes sweeping the locker room until they fell on Jed.

"Hey, Jed!" Charlie called, heading towards him. "So what's new?"

"You know I don't talk to reporters, Huff. Get lost."

"You talked to Connie Kenyon," Charlie said. "And I know it. Vinnie fired her because she refused to write some story about you. She may be sweet on you, Duval, but I'm not. I'm going to find out what it is and I'll smear it all over the sports page, front page, anything it takes. Why not do yourself a favor? Come clean with me and I'll go easy on you. If you're in some kind of trouble, I'll help you, okay? I'll write a sympathetic story. You just gotta trust me, Jed. I'll do right by you."

Jed stared at Charlie as he talked, and as he listened everything clicked into place. Suddenly everything was clear. Still, he wanted to be absolutely sure he understood. "Con was fired?"

"Yeah." Charlie sidled up to Jed, talking out of the side of his mouth. "I guess she's smitten with you,

Jed, which is good she didn't write the story, because a woman in love is stupid. But you gotta be careful. You break it off with her, she'll get mad and write the damn story. That's why you should talk to me, come clean, let's get this thing out in the open before she gets angry enough to do a hatchet job on you."

"You think she'd do that, Charlie?" Jed asked, widening his eyes in pretended country-boy innocence. "You think she'd actually do a hatchet job on me?"

"If she's mad enough. Hell, Duval, you can't trust a woman, especially a career woman. All they think about is their work."

Jed stared at Charlie, feeling revulsion begin deep in his gut and travel up his chest, as if he were going to throw up. But he didn't know who was more repulsive—Charlie Huff or himself. What a fool he'd been. Con had promised him she wouldn't write the story and she'd kept her promise, even in the face of losing her job.

He felt sick, bereft, as if he'd just found out that the person he'd turned on was the person who'd once saved his life. And here was Charlie Huff, bloated with self-serving ambition, ready to stab Con in the back in order to get Jed's story for himself.

He shook his head as if to clear it and stared down at the floor. Sometimes he just wanted to walk away from life. He wanted to go back to the minor leagues, when all that mattered was pitching, when there hadn't been any fame or money or glory. Life had been simple then.

He felt as if he were living a terrible lie, pretending to be a hero when he had enormous feet of clay. He wasn't even man enough to tell the world he couldn't read. And meanwhile, Con had bared her soul to the world, sharing a past that was much grimmer than his.

He sat down abruptly, Charlie Huff all but forgotten. All that mattered now was the new information about Con, and his sickening realization that she cared for him more than he'd ever suspected, enough to lose her job to protect him.

And he'd been angry because she didn't have time to teach him to read.

He dropped his head into his hands, staring at the floor. He was a fool, a certifiable Class *A* jerk.

Charlie Huff grinned slyly. "Hey, Jed, it's not that bad," he said in a low voice. "No matter what you're hiding, it'll feel better when you come clean and it's out in the open. Boston's a forgiving town, Jed. The fans might be shocked at first, but look at how most of them have forgiven Pete Rose."

Charlie put a friendly arm around Jed's shoulder. "Is what you're hiding worse than what Pete did, or better? I mean, can you give me an estimate here? Are we talkin' stealing, a prison term, rape?"

Jed stood up and pushed past Charlie Huff. "Get out of my way," he snarled. "You make me sick."

He walked without seeing anyone or anything. All that mattered was getting to Con, telling her he was sorry, that he understood now what she'd done for him. He just hoped she'd be able to forgive him. He wouldn't blame her if she couldn't. His stomach felt sick and his heart was hammering as he raced to the Blazer. But then he realized he didn't even know where she lived.

He looked around the parking lot, and it hit him all at once—his complete helplessness at finding her. He couldn't read a map to get to Meecham. He couldn't read a phone book to look up the small newspaper in Meecham where Con now worked. He didn't have her new phone number. She was gone, lost, and all because he had been too proud to admit he couldn't read, and too afraid to try to learn.

He leaned back against the Blazer, utterly defeated. It was the lowest point of his life, the place he'd forced himself into while trying to hold his life together with Band-Aids and Scotch tape. Anything rather than admit he needed help. He'd rather starve, or even die, than admit he couldn't read, that he had a problem.

Stiff-necked pride and a weak ego, they were his biggest flaws. He wondered if Con realized that about him, if that's why she'd turned her back on him and left him. Had she recognized that, despite his winning pitching record, he was really a loser?

He looked up and saw Charlie Huff walking toward him. He felt the old revulsion ripple through him, felt like belting Charlie Huff, sending him straight to the moon, as good old Jackie Gleason used to say.

"Hey, Jed," Charlie puffed as he drew near him, "glad you reconsidered. It never does any good to run away. Stay and face the music, son. It might not be much fun, but it'll blow over. Look at Con. Use her as an example. No one in Boston wanted to talk to her after she published that story, but it'll all be forgotten in a few months."

"Why did she publish that story?" Jed asked. It had never occurred to him to ask before. He'd been too fixated on his own problems.

Charlie miscalculated. He figured Jed didn't care about Con. Laughing, he leaned back against the Blazer. "Well, you see, what happened was this . . ." He snickered again, remembering his role in Con's story's getting written. "I started checking up on our little Con when she got interested in horning in on my territory. It didn't take long to find the truth about who she really is."

He grinned. "So I says to her, you don't tell me Jed's story, I'm writin' all this for the good readers of the *Courier*, blowin' your cover, so to speak." Charlie laughed out loud. "Fooled me, though. She wrote it herself. But she's off the paper now and that's all that matters. Now let's get down to brass tacks, Jed. What's this story you've been hiding for so long?''

He turned to Jed in time to meet a balled-up fist straight in the nose. Surprise gave way to unconsciousness. He slid to the ground, completely out.

Jed got in the Blazer and drove away.

"CAN YOU TELL ME how to get Meecham?" Jed asked a pedestrian on the sidewalk about a block from Barons Park.

"Never heard of it."

He accelerated and stopped farther down the road. "Can you tell me how to get Meecham?"

"Let's see, Meecham. Okay, you take 128 North and go up toward Peabody—" He pronounced it "Peabiddy," the way everyone in Massachusetts did. "But you get off before Peabody. Go toward Saugus. It's around there somewhere. You'll see the signs."

Jed thanked him, thinking, "I'll see the signs, but I won't be able to read them."

He knew from experience, though, that he could find his way. He had the illiterate's determination, that half-spunky, half-fearful knowledge that he could get there blindfolded, because he had to, almost literally. The person who could read had no idea what it was like, trying to navigate through a world that depended so completely on the written word.

What would take most people an hour took Jed three hours, but he found Meecham. Then he was faced with the task of finding the newspaper.

"Can you tell me where the local newspaper is?" he asked.

"Over on Dowd," someone said.

"Can you tell me where that is?"

The person gave him a detailed explanation, but halfway there he got lost and had to ask someone else. Then he took a wrong turn and had to ask someone else.

Finally he found it. He parked the Blazer and stared at the small building with its large plate-glass window with the indecipherable letters on the window.

He got out and approached the door, then hesitated. What would he say? He hadn't even had time to think. Then he realized this was no time to stop and think. He'd never used his head before in his entire life, why start now?

He opened the door and walked in. An elderly woman with blue hair looked up over her glass frames. "Yes? Can I help you?"

"Is Con Kenyon here?"

"No, I'm sorry, she's out of the office right now. Can I leave her a message?"

"Can you tell me where she lives?"

"I'm afraid not, sir. That's against company policy."

"But I'm a friend of hers."

"You could be her cousin, but I'm not giving out her home address," the old lady said fiercely. "Now that's that, young man."

He sighed and looked around. It wasn't much to look at. There were a few small cubicles that he guessed served as offices and some anemic plants that looked like they lived on pure willpower.

"Would you like to leave her a note?" the old lady asked, relenting a little.

"I'd like to, ma'am," he said, "but I can't write."

She stared at him, her mouth dropping open. "Oh, I'm so sorry." She looked embarrassed and suddenly didn't seem to know where to look. He didn't know who felt worse—her or him. "Maybe you could write something down for me," he said.

"Why, of course!" She got a pad of paper and a pen. "What would you like to say?"

He was stumped. What did he want to say? I'm sorry? Forgive me? He stared at the floor, trying to formulate thoughts. "Um, maybe you could just say Jed Duval was here."

"Jed Duval," she said out loud, writing quickly. "Okay, anything else?"

"And I . . . I'd sure like her to call me when she gets a chance. I need to talk to her very bad. It's very important."

"Is it an emergency?" the old lady asked, raising a gray eyebrow inquisitively.

"Well, it sure feels like one," Jed said.

"An emergency," the old lady said, writing it down. "Does she have your phone number?"

"Yes, ma'am, but you can take it down just in case." He gave it to her, then thanked her and turned to go.

"I'll see Con gets this, Mr. Duval."

"Thank you," he said, turning back to smile at the old lady.

She smiled back. "Have a good day."

"Yes, ma'am, I'll try to."

"You could wait around if you like. I expect Con back within a half an hour."

"You do?" He felt his spirits rise. "Well, maybe I'll just go over to that shop and have a cup of coffee."

"You do that," the old lady said, smiling. "Then come on back in a half an hour or so."

He sprinted across the street and took a seat in an empty booth in the small coffee shop. He ordered coffee and a hamburger, then sat back to wait.

He'd be in trouble with management, he realized. He'd left Barons Field without showing up for practice, which on the Barons was a punishable offense. He'd be fined a day's pay, but he didn't care if they took a month's pay away from him. Con mattered more than anything.

He sipped his coffee and ate the thin hamburger, wondering how the place stayed in business serving food this bad. He kept his eyes on the newspaper office across the street, waiting for any sign of Con appearing in her car or on foot. He studied the newspaper office, noting how worn-down it seemed. The entire town of Meecham was a mess, just as she'd described it in the article she'd read out loud to him.

He sighed and wondered if she would have ever told him the truth if he hadn't stumbled on it himself. Probably not. Con was as stubborn and proud in her way as he was in his.

Then he saw her. She had pulled up to the curb in her little car and she was getting out. She looked terrific, wearing a pair of faded jeans and a white peasant-type blouse. Her hair was as golden as ever. She wasn't smiling, but she looked okay. Better than okay. She looked wonderful.

He left a five-dollar bill on the table and went across the street. "Con?"

She heard her name and turned around. When she saw him, her face changed. Hope seemed to fill her eyes. Without thinking, she smiled. "Jed. What brings you out here?"

"We need to talk."

She looked around. "Well, okay."

"Could we go back to your place? If you're finished with work, that is?"

She glanced at her watch. "I've just got a couple things to do, but I'll be out in five minutes. You can follow me home."

"All right. I'll wait here."

She nodded, her face serious. Turning, she walked into the office.

Chapter Nineteen

Con's apartment was on the outskirts of Meecham. The building had all the charm of a bowling alley built in the 1950s. But her apartment was neat and clean, and what it lacked in architectural charm, she made up for with her bookcases filled with books, her oriental carpet, the botanical prints matted in marbled paper and encased in slender gold frames. The couch was piled high with chintz pillows. Stacks of books and magazines sat on an antique pine trunk that served as a coffee table.

"I'll make some ice tea," she said, and headed for the kitchen.

"It's not much," she said, noticing the way he looked around, "but I'm planning on fixing it up. I'm going to strip the wallpaper this weekend and take off that ugly paneling."

"Con."

She didn't turn around. She was trembling and she didn't want him to know it. "What?"

"Con, I know you had to leave the *Courier.*"

Her heart stopped. She kept her eyes down, her hands steady. "What do you mean?"

Jed reached out and put a gentle hand on her arm and turned her to face him. "Con," he said gently. "Come here."

She went into his arms and everything was a blur. The whole world was tears and she was shaking, but his arms felt like the safest place in the world, the kindest shelter, the most loving harbor. She couldn't stop the tears; they ran down her face and she was sobbing and all she could do was hold on to him, cling to him and hold on tight, because if she let go, she was going to be lost. Lately, it had felt that bad, that scary, that lonely. And his arms felt that good.

"Con," he said, stroking her hair, cradling her against him. "It's okay."

She shook her head, her tears pouring down her face like rain gushing from gray clouds. "I don't know why I'm crying."

"I do," he said, leading her to the living room couch. "Come on, sit down. Let's just talk."

At last she was able to stop crying. She felt like such a complete fool. She took a shaky breath and wiped her face and realized that her mascara was running and she must look like a clown. "I feel so stupid."

"I'm the one who's stupid," he said quietly.

She shook her head, her eyes filled with pain. "No, Jed. Don't ever say that." She reached out and touched his hand. "Why are you here? Is anything wrong?"

He looked into her eyes and shook his head wonderingly. "This is just like you, to worry about me when you've lost everything because of me."

"I haven't lost everything," she said, gesturing around her. "I have this."

"Some great place," he said softly, but he was smiling at her.

She smiled back. "Hey, it's a roof over my head. That's more than lots of people have these days."

He stared at her, needing to drink in her eyes and mouth and nose, her hair, her shoulders. He needed to memorize her expressions and imprint her face in his mind so that if he ever had to leave her, she'd be there so fast in his memory that he'd be able to call her image up in a moment's notice, to remember her in total and accurate detail.

"I've been such a damn fool," he said heavily. "I can't believe I believed Charlie Huff over you."

"How'd you find out you couldn't?" she asked softly.

"He came up to me in the clubhouse today, bragging about how you were out of the picture now and how I should be glad because I'd never be able to trust you. The guy is such a slime."

"It's about time you figured that out, Jed Duval!"

"I couldn't believe it when he told me that you'd had to leave the paper because you wouldn't write that story. And there I'd been sitting in the locker room feeling sorry for myself because you hadn't had the time to teach me to read."

Her eyes were filled with love as she watched him. It hurt her to see him hurting. It's funny how there wasn't any real payoff to hearing him say he'd been wrong about her. Why didn't she fell triumphant, vindicated? Why wasn't she rejoicing in her victory?

She supposed because it didn't really matter. All that mattered was Jed. She guessed that was what love was about.

"Stop being so hard on yourself. Don't you think I understood that you couldn't trust me? I'm not stupid, you know."

"But I am!" he said fiercely, self-revulsion filling him like bile.

She shook her head. Reaching out, she took his hand. "No, you're not."

Something in her voice made him look up at her. "But—" She shook her head. She was so certain she was right, he had to stop his protests and just stare at her. He couldn't argue in the face of the confidence she displayed in him.

"The man I love isn't stupid," she said softly.

He felt the strangest feeling in his chest. And in his stomach, too. Everywhere, in fact. All inside himself. The strangest warmest, most wonderful feeling, like someone had showered gold dust on him, making him feel warm inside, and good. Just plain good.

It was her eyes that got him. They were the warmest eyes he'd ever seen in his life, and filled with so much love he felt as if he were choking on his feelings. He was filled up with good things, filled to the brim and overflowing with happy feelings, good feelings, the kind of feelings he didn't ever remember feeling in his entire life.

"So this is what love is," he said, smiling.

She nodded, her eyes shining. Somehow, she knew things were going to be all right.

"I'm sorry, Con," he said, looking into her eyes, his face suddenly serious. "I am so very sorry."

"It's okay," she whispered.

And then she was in his arms and he didn't know if he'd taken her there, or if she'd gone into them just as he opened them up. They were together and they were holding each other and nothing else on earth seemed to matter remotely as much—not baseball or pitching or a five-million-dollar contract or Jade Island or anything. Just Con and him, together, holding each other.

"Oh, Con," he whispered. "I love you."

She closed her eyes. There it was. What she'd longed for for so long and hadn't even known she'd longed for. Those words, this moment, when she knew that everything would be okay, no matter what else went wrong.

"I am the luckiest man in the world," he said quietly. "To know that in all the world, I found you, just stumbled on you. It's as if I knew right from the start, but couldn't let myself believe it. I kept fighting you." He smiled. "Because you were a reporter."

"Your dreaded enemy."

"Why did you do it? Why did you sacrifice your career for me? I can't let you do that, Con."

"I didn't sacrifice it, Jed. I made a move I had to make in order to live by my principles. Vinnie wouldn't trust me to do what I felt was right. He wanted the story and I told him he'd get it, but only when you were ready to have it published. That wasn't good enough for him, but it's the only way I can operate, Jed. I gave you a promise and nothing on God's green earth was going to make me break that promise. It was my word, Jed, and that means something. Maybe not to Vinnie, but it does to me."

"But if I hadn't been so thickheaded, none of this would have happened."

"Jed, you did what you felt you had to. I hid my real past from you because I was scared to tell you about it, scared of what you'd think of me. You've been hiding the fact that you can't read. Big deal. I'll bet a lot of people hide things. It's part of being human. Stop blasting yourself for being who you are. There's nothing wrong with you, just the way you are."

Her words were like a blessing. He felt them seep deep into his bones. She loved him, Jed Duval, a man who couldn't read.

No, that wasn't really right, a man who was too afraid to try to learn. He'd met every battle in his life with courage and fortitude except the one that meant the most. He'd run and hidden, scurried under the rug like a frightened mouse. All to keep from having to face what he feared so much: he couldn't learn to read.

He swallowed. "I guess I need to call those Literacy Volunteer people," he said at last.

"That would be a good idea."

He looked up at her. She was smiling at him, her eyes filled with warmth and love and something else, something he suddenly recognized as faith. She believed in him. She was utterly without fear that he could learn to read. She knew he could. There was just no way he couldn't. He saw that in her eyes and in her smile.

"Then maybe you better write that story."

"Are you sure? Don't you want to wait? Get a few lessons under your belt?"

He shook his head. "I think it'd be a lot easier to go into the Literacy Volunteers program knowing I don't have to hide anymore. Maybe I can help a lot of other people by having my story come out, Con. I'll bet there are others who are afraid, too, who live the same kind of narrow life I've lived, not believing in themselves."

"The problem is, we're going to have to find a way to get that story to them," she said. "That means radio and television, Jed, lots of it. Going on talk shows and talking about it. Maybe even going to schools, to catch the kids before they leave school. Are you willing to do that kind of thing? Because if you really want to make a difference, if you really want to help others, that's what it would take. Lots of hard work and dedication."

"I guess that's the only thing I can do," he said quietly. "I'll always love baseball. I'll pitch as long as I can. Someday I want to be in the Hall of Fame. But that's not everything. You've shown me that. For a life to really matter, you have to face your fears, come to terms with them, then turn around and help someone else who's fighting the same battle you are."

"That's why I'm in Meecham and not Beacon Hill. They don't need me. The people in Meecham do. There's a story I'm working on now?" She sat up, excited. She wanted to tell him everything. "It's about high-school drop-outs. Jed, you wouldn't believe these kids...."

He smiled and sat back and listened. He loved to see her eyes glowing with enthusiasm. He loved to hear her talk about fighting injustice and giving these kids hope, about writing what she needed to write, deep in her heart, about things that really mattered.

Someday he was going to marry her, when he could read the marriage license and decipher all the mean-

ings of the words in the wedding ceremony. And he·
was going to love her the way she loved him—for
whom she was, supporting her in everything she
needed and desire.

Epilogue

It was late October. Vibrantly colored leaves fluttered gently to the ground, carpeting the lawn outside the small chapel on the outskirts of Meecham. The air was crisp, the sky deep blue. Just four days earlier, the Boston Barons had won the World Series. Jed had pitched the seventh game—a shutout for the final victory.

Inside the chapel candles flickered, throwing soft shadows on the walls. Organ music played softly in the background. The guests shuffled their feet, coughed and whispered among themselves. They all agreed—there had never been a more beautiful bride.

Dressed in ivory satin, a lace veil covering her hair, Con stood with her hand in Jed's, her eyes smiling with love, as she looked at him as he prepared to read the words of their wedding ceremony.

The words swam before Jed's eyes, then everything became clear. What had once been just smudges on a page were now clear to him, decipherable. He realized that nothing in his life had ever been as precious as this moment. In a clear voice, he began to read out loud:

In the name of God, I, Jed, take you, Constance, to be my wife, to have and to hold from this day forward, for better or worse, for richer or poorer, in sickness and health, to love and to cherish, until we are parted by death. This is my solemn vow...

COMING NEXT MONTH

#453 RAFE'S REVENGE by Anne Stuart

In Hollywood, where only winners survived, Rafe McGinnis was known as a fighter who never gave up. And neither did film critic Silver Carlysle. Theirs was a battle of wills—but each new skirmish only fueled their mutual desire. Despite the danger, Silver couldn't surrender. For Rafe had laid out his terms: Nothing less than a night in her arms would satisfy him.

#454 ONCE UPON A TIME by Rebecca Flanders

With buccaneer blood in his veins and a savage thirst for adventure, Chris Vandermere loomed like a modern-day pirate to his sassy stowaway, Lanie Robinson. She thought such men lived only in her dreams, but then she met Chris's lips and fantasy threatened to become reality.

#455 SAND MAN by Tracy Hughes

Like the Sand Man of her childhood dreams, Jake Abel brought a special magic into Maggie Conrad's life. Jake was anything but a myth. When he sprinkled his magic dust, Maggie almost believed that wishes could come true—despite their differences. But Jake was unstoppable and he'd made up his mind. He wanted Maggie in his life... and in his bed.

#456 THE COWBOY'S MISTRESS by Cathy Gillen Thacker

In the battle for the Bar W Ranch, Travis Wescott employed his devilish, double-edged tongue—using one side for witty repartee and the other for kissing his flame-haired adversary, Rachel. She meant to show him no one could rein in her ambition. And now Travis dreamed of claiming his ranch and branding Rachel his forever.

HARLEQUIN
American Romance®

American Romance's year-long celebration continues.... Join your favorite authors as they celebrate love set against the special times each month throughout 1992.

Next month... If Maggie knew college men looked this good, she'd've gone back to school years ago. Now forty and about to become a grandma, can she handle these sexy young men? Find out in:

SEPTEMBER

**SAND MAN
by Tracy Hughes**

Read all the Calendar of Romance titles, coming to you one per month, all year, only in American Romance.